Praise For Pete Altieri

"An absolute page-turner! I couldn't put this book down! Pete Altieri's stories are dark and extremely disturbing, which means a lot coming from me!" Tony Campagna, Spellbound FX and Art

"Pete's storytelling is phenomenal. I've found myself caught up in the incredible sense of dread that builds as his pieces progress. His attention to detail in both characters and setting is brilliant and lends his stories a tangible sense of reality and weight. Pete's ideas are original, and no two stories are alike, keeping me on my toes the whole time. The dark corners of my house will never look the same again!" Shaun Farrugia, artist/musician

"Pete Altieri is a great writer. I read both, The Creep and The Last Supper, loved them both. They are right up there beside my two favorite authors, Jack Ketchum and the early works of Stephen King." Jeff Gaither, artist

"I met Pete as a podcaster and fellow fan of horror but know him best through his amazing writing. His ability to weave a macabre tale is in line with some of the great names in the industry. Whether the reader is looking for a light scare or a deep dive into the dark recesses of the human soul, his stories will tantalize and terrify." Brad Tucker, podcaster and voice actor

"In another installment from thriller mastermind Pete Altieri, he leaves nothing behind except the reader's sanity. The terror felt in his previous books has been ramped up to a nightmarish fever pitch, you not only will leave the lights on, but you will try and sleep with a weapon beside your bed. His tales of terror are threaded with Poe and Lovecraftian expertise ripped straight from the days of gothic horror." Amanda Howard, author and podcaster

Other Books by Pete Altieri on
Blunt Force Press

Short Story Collections

Creation of Chaos: Volume I
Creation of Chaos: Volume II
Creation of Chaos: Volume III

Novels

*Deeper Than Dead (illustrated
by Brian Uziel)*

*The Dreadful Lives of Enoch
Strange*

Slab of Sickness: Terror on the Tracks

Pete Altieri

Blunt Force Press

For the readers who enjoy taking twisted journeys with me and not screaming too loud.

Table of Contents

Slab of Sickness:
Terror on the
Tracks

Serving Up the Slab

Welcome to the first of my new series, *Slab of Sickness*! This is an idea that came up in a dinner conversation with my wife and editor, Jenny. We were discussing the stories, *The 666 Express* and *Create the Chaos*. She thought it would be a good idea to release them together since they are intended to be a back-to-back infernal experience. I agreed with her and that started things in motion – terror on the tracks!

I was working on *Death of a Resurrection Man* and decided to add it to the collection and publish the three stories under a new series. The *Slab of Sickness* series will be something I plan to release between projects to give you readers something to nibble on while you're waiting for the next main course. Think of them like breadsticks or fried ravioli with some marinara sauce. You get the idea.

Slab of Sickness is a saying I used in my years playing in a metal band and doing album reviews for others. For example, "this latest slab of sickness is a killer album from (insert band name)". I like the sound of it and figured it would go well with the stories that you are about to read. I asked some of my friends about the name and they seemed to like it, too. I think it has a nice ring to it and warns the readers they are about to embark on a dark and twisted journey. No one can claim ignorance with a title like that!

Brian Uziel, who has done nearly all the artwork for my books, suggested grindhouse style art for the covers in the series. I thought it was a great idea and different from the other projects we've worked on before. He's got a great eye and vision to accompany my writing, which is why we've done so many projects together. Brian and I recently spent a couple days at a horror convention and talked quite a bit about the projects and came up with what you are looking at right now.

I have several ideas for other collections like this I can do with common themes. For example, my short stories *Follow* and *The Bells of San Pedro* share a character who likes to pretend he's something he's not. I can easily write a third story and make it a *Slab of Sickness*. Or possibly an all-Poe homage, since I wrote the story, *The Tell-Tale Heart,* with my twist on it as *The Eyes Have It.* Or what about Lovecraft stories, since I already wrote my version of *The Thing On the Doorstep*? I also would love to pay tribute to other authors I like in the genre like Robert Bloch and Ray Bradbury. The possibilities are endless.

The 666 Express was originally published in *Creation of Chaos III,* but I decided if I was going include it with this collection, I would change the ending and give the story a bit of a once over. I called it the 2022 sizzling ending. I did make very minor changes to the original but gave it a completely new ending. If you liked the original story, then I hope you like this new end to the fiery tale!

Create the Chaos was written as a sequel to *The 666 Express,* including the same characters based on my real life co-hosts of the *Murder Metal Mayhem* podcast. I needed to come up with a way to address the death of our co-host, Chris "CK" Kovacs, since he passed in October of 2021. That was after I wrote *The 666 Express* and before I started

Create The Chaos. I also wanted to introduce a new character to the action and decided that Shaun Farrugia would be fun to join the ensemble. I watched a documentary on how they dug the subway in New York City, and it inspired the idea of unearthing a terrible evil that is let loose on the characters. I plan to write other stories using these real-life characters, and the fact we die at the end of each one would be a recurring theme.

Death of a Resurrection Man was written after I watched a few documentaries about the infamous body snatchers turned serial killers, William Burke and William Hare, in 1820s Edinburgh, Scotland. I did a lot of research about them for one of our podcast episodes and decided to write a story about resurrection men. I devised a ghastly Dr. Goolsbee to be at the epicenter of this dark tale set in that time. His last name is intentionally ghoulish, like his personality. I read the diary of a resurrection man who lived in 19th century London, who kept detailed notes of his business providing cadavers to surgeons for medical research. I used a map of Sheffield, England from the 1820s so I could reference real street names and locations. Some of the details are real but much of it is fiction. Blending the two is something I really like to do. I found the whole concept fascinating, and I think you'll enjoy this dark story with some interesting characters.

Well, enough of the introductions. Let's get to the meat of the situation and enjoy a bit of this slab of sickness together! Can you pass the steak sauce?

Pete Altieri – Heyworth, Illinois
September 2022

The 666 Express
(2022 sizzling ending)

"Win a ride on The 666 Express!" said a young man in a devil costume, complete with a realistic pointed tail, long twisted horns, and a red skin tone. He was standing outside the Railroad Spike Saloon passing out fliers on red paper.

Patrons of the bar were filing out after a heavy metal show at the venue in Dallas, Texas. The Australian band, In Malice's Wake, was on tour with two US national acts and a local Fort Worth band, Slowly You Die. The realistic devil costume got the attention desired, plus it didn't hurt that his two attractive 19-year-old female assistants were each wearing an extremely short red leather skirt with a devil tail, a tight cleavage-revealing bustier, and thigh-high shiny black boots. Each of the girls were holding pitchforks in one hand and their fliers in the other. They smiled as the male-dominated crowd were more than willing to grab a flier from the sexy devilish assistants.

"Win a ride on The 666 Express!" the man dressed like the Devil said again as the crowd continued to leave the venue.

"Man, that was one hell of a good show!" Chris said, taking one of the fliers.

"What is that?" Pete said, looking over Chris' shoulder as he held up the red flier that read:

TAKE A RIDE ON THE 666 EXPRESS!
Win two FREE tickets on the maiden voyage of a new
state-of-the-art train.
Ride the 666 Express and travel 666 miles per hour,
from Dallas to Denver, in 1 hour!

There was a website address at the bottom and a QR code that could be scanned with a cell phone.

"I'm not sure. Some flier for a new train called The 666 Express," Chris answered, a bit of skepticism in his voice. He passed the flier to Pete, who was also doubtful.

"Sounds like a scam. Maybe it's a new band or something? Who the hell names a train The 666 Express?" Pete added. "It sounds bad ass, though!"

"Yeah, if it's real," Chris said.

As the two friends walked to their car in the nearby parking deck on 14th Street, Pete scanned the QR code with his phone.

"Well, it looks like the flier is right. This website says they're giving away two tickets for the first trip on this new train that travels 666 miles an hour. That's crazy! It would take you 12 hours to drive to Denver on a good day," Pete said as they approached Chris' Nissan Sentra.

Chris laughed as they got into the car.

"Sounds crazy. I didn't realize Denver was 666 miles from Dallas. This train says it can get you there in an hour? Sounds like bullshit to me."

Pete laughed also, but entered his name, email address, and verified that he wasn't a robot on the website form and pressed enter.

"There, we're entered. It says if you win, you get two tickets. I doubt it. I never win anything."

Chris started the car. In Malice's Wake was cranked up on the stereo since they had been playing the latest album on the way to the show, a tradition of theirs. The two went to heavy metal shows all the time. Friends since high school, the 45-year-old men were still young at heart.

"Who knows? Someone's gotta win those tickets. Maybe we'll get lucky," Chris said, backing out of the parking spot.

"True. We'll see, I guess."

Pete turned up the stereo and they bobbed their heads to the music.

*****

Chris and Pete were sitting in the living room of Chris' two-bedroom apartment, where he lived with his wife, Laura. Chris used the second bedroom to store his massive CD and vinyl collection that had grown out of control with the invention of online shopping and two-day shipping. When Chris and Pete started their podcast, *Heavy Metal Mayhem*, they needed a place to record it. Chris moved his collection into the attic and renovated the room for a studio. They had been doing the podcast almost a year and it was slowly improving. The biggest struggle for two middle-aged men to understand was the technical side of things, but they managed to get the studio set up to record and produce the show. The main thing was they loved talking about their favorite subject – heavy metal music. It gave them both an escape from their otherwise serious lives to a world where mosh pits and stage diving were king. They would have gladly done the podcast every week even if people weren't listening.

Pete came by every Tuesday after work to record the episodes. He was working at a local manufacturing plant as their safety and health manager. He'd been there 21 years and was making good money with excellent benefits. He and his long-time girlfriend, Jennifer, lived in a small one-bedroom apartment in downtown Dallas. They had been saving up for a house since they were to get married the next Spring. So, Pete moved in with Jennifer, and they planned to share the small apartment until they had enough to put up a big down payment. Jennifer was an office manager at a local community college. She didn't share Pete's taste in music, so, on Tuesday nights, she stayed home and worked in her garden or on an art project. Their cat, Scarlett, kept her company when she was at the apartment alone.

Laura tolerated the noise the guys made when they got together. She was happy for Chris to have kept a friend since high school. Most people lose touch. But Pete and Chris graduated together in 1990 and kept going to concerts, hanging out on the weekends, and listening to heavy metal. Chris got his PhD in the Fall and was now a professor of biology at Clemmons College, a private school in Fort Worth that was a think tank for young scientific minds. Laura enjoyed her job as a high school art teacher. She and Jennifer would sometimes get together on Tuesday nights while the guys recorded the podcast. They both liked 60s and 70s music, and a penchant for all kinds of art, so they often worked on projects together.

Pete heard a familiar beep sound from his cell phone. The guys were going over a few notes about the podcast they were getting ready to record to make sure there were no questions. He picked up the phone from the coffee table.

"Holy shit! I can't believe it!" he said, staring at his phone.

"What's up, man?" Chris asked, still looking down at the notes for the podcast.

"Hang on a second," Pete said, scrolling down on his phone, reading something.

"Is something wrong at home, bro? A work thing?" Chris said.

"No. I just got a text message from Diablo Productions, about that 666 Express train."

Chris was dumbfounded. He forgot all about The 666 Express and the man in the strange devil costume from a week ago.

"What? That's crazy! Did you win?" Chris asked, setting his notes aside.

"I have to call this phone number."

"Well, call it! What the hell are you waiting for? We can tell all our listeners we're going on the 666 Express! They'll love it. Maybe we'll get more than a hundred listens this week, finally!" Chris said, taking a long drink from his beer.

Pete looked over at Chris in disbelief. He couldn't believe he may have won the tickets. It felt as if he were in a dream, but he clicked on the phone number provided in the text message from Diablo Productions.

"Is it ringing?" Chris asked, his eyes alive with wonder.

"Yeah." He put the call on speaker. It rang a second time. Then a third.

"Damn, I knew it was too good to be true," Pete said, dejected.

"Good evening. Thank you for calling Diablo Productions. Home of the 666 Express!" a booming male voice said. Chris and Pete were startled, listening to it on speaker phone.

"Yes, I just got a text message from you," Pete said, feeling jittery with excitement.

"Yes, you've won two tickets on The 666 Express! Congratulations! You will get an email with detailed instructions," the man said.

"Hell yeah, that sounds awesome!" Pete said, Chris was giving him a high-five.

"The train leaves on Saturday morning at 10:30. Be at the North Dallas train station at 9. All the details will be in the email that we'll send out in the next couple days. We look forward to seeing you and your guest! Congratulations, once again!"

"Thank you!" Pete and Chris said together.

They spent the entire podcast hour talking about their upcoming trip on The 666 Express and played as many heavy metal songs as they could come up with that had references to the ominous three-digit number. Despite the foreboding feelings some would have expressed at the thought of riding The 666 Express, they were excited beyond belief. Jennifer and Laura were happy for them. Life couldn't get any better than this.

*****

It was just after 9am on Saturday as Chris and Pete made their way across the parking lot of the North Dallas train station. It was packed full of cars and people hanging out in groups like it was a tailgate party before a heavy metal show. Everyone had on their favorite black concert shirt on, and as the two made their way toward the train, the familiar smell of marijuana was in the air, and metal was cranking on all the stereos. Despite the fact it was only 9am, most of the people in the parking lot were drinking beer and partying like it was a Friday night. Although Chris and Pete were older than most of the people there, they felt at home with fans of the music they loved for 30 years. They were definitely not the average heavy metal fans, especially Chris with his PhD, but they were in familiar territory.

They followed the signs that read "The 666 Express" and made their way toward the train platform. Pete had the tickets on his phone. After reading the email that he got from Diablo Productions, he had to electronically sign a release form that said he couldn't sue them if anything happened on the train ride. He thought nothing of the legal talk, and the tickets were sent to him electronically. No one had heard of The 666 Express, but it sounded "metal" and "evil" and that's all most fans of heavy metal music needed. They both joked about getting tickets to the first trip of the new train, drawing the obvious parallels to the disastrous maiden voyage of the Titanic.

Chris and Pete could see a large crowd of about 500 people gather around a podium that was set up on the train station platform, with a large backdrop behind it that read, "Ride The 666 Express!". There were flames painted around it. Heavy metal music was playing over a public address system as the crowd became anxious the closer it got to 10am, when the train was supposed to be boarding for a 10:30 departure. They were only a few people from the very front of the crowd, and they could feel the push behind them as more of the ticket winners shoved their way closer to the stage.

"I can't get over the crowd here. It's like we're at a metal show," Pete said as he braced himself, the push behind him getting stronger.

"For sure. This is so cool. Thanks for giving me the extra ticket!" Chris said, taking in the excitement of the moment.

Suddenly the music over the public address system faded and dry ice began to pour in from around and under the banner. The crowd let out a cheer and an instrumental metal song with a driving beat began over the sound system. It was a song they hadn't heard before, and that was saying something due to the hard rock and heavy metal acumen they each possessed. From the smoke emerged the figure of the man dressed in the devil costume they saw outside the venue after the concert. He was smiling big and looking over the crowd cheering wildly before him.

"Thank you all for coming here on this fine Saturday

morning!" the man said into the microphone. As the smoke cleared, they could see Diablo Productions wood-burned into the front of the dark mahogany podium he stood behind.

The crowd continued to cheer, and the driving music quieted a bit.

"You have all been selected to take this historic ride today on The 666 Express. A modern wonder that will take you on a one-hour ride from Dallas to Denver – riding at a neck-breaking 666 miles an hour!" the man said with obvious oratory skill. "Together, we'll make history! If this is a success, you'll see The 666 Express in other parts of the United States, Canada, and in Europe."

Pete was marveling at the instant command the man had over the crowd. Everyone was cheering and staring at him like a rock star. Many had their hands up, either clenched fists or showing "the horns" with the heavy metal sign that all fans of the genre knew. It was incredible to see. Pete looked around both sides of him in amazement.

"Here in a few minutes, we will open up the platform. Please move in an orderly fashion to the lovely ladies that await you, so your tickets can be scanned in. You will have to check in your cell phones, cameras, and any other personal items with our staff, so they can be secured for the hour-long trip. They will be promptly returned to you when we reach Denver. We don't want any pictures or video to leak out on social media. I'm sure you understand. This is a special trip on the maiden voyage. Our staff will take you to your assigned seating once your personal items have been secured. This will need to happen quickly so we can achieve our 10:30 am departure for arrival in Denver one hour later." The man smiled once again at the crowd, walked to the left side of the banner, and out of sight as the dry ice began to dissipate behind him.

As Chris and Pete made their way down the platform,

they could see the sunshine gleaming off the incredible blood red train with "The 666 Express" painted on the side, complete with flames and a laughing devil face. There was a row of black tinted windows that were only two feet high and spanned the length of the train cars. According to the email that went out, there were ten cars and a total of 40 people on each. There was a locomotive car at the front that provided all the power, and it was also red with flames going down each side. There appeared to be a large, tinted windshield at the front but no obvious way in or out. The train design was sleek and very modern looking and appeared to be ready for the challenge of crushing the speed record for a passenger train, previously set in Tokyo, Japan at slightly over 300 miles per hour.

There was a huge banner that hung across the platform that read "Ride The 666 Express Maiden Voyage and Make History!". There were at least a dozen women dressed up like the devilish assistants from the In Malice's Wake concert standing near the banner, scanning tickets, and directing the patrons to their assigned seating. There was a steady cloud of dry ice coming from behind the women and made the display that much more like going to a concert. Heavy metal music was coming through the train station sound system. The ticket winners and their guests filtered onto the trains, marveling at the pomp and circumstance of the entire experience.

Pete took out his cell phone with the tickets as one of the women scanned it with a hand-held device. Additional female staff in the devil costumes were in each of the train cars, checking in personal items. Pete and Chris got their assigned seating in the back row of the first car. There was an aisle and two seats on each side. There were only ten rows of seats, so it was extremely comfortable, with plenty of leg room for forty passengers. The seats were black leather with the interior walls the same blood red that the trains were painted in. The windows seemed tinted on both sides, making visibility difficult even from inside. There was a 60-inch video screen at the front of the car, facing the patrons. It was scrolling various messages about the train and some of the facts about the trip they were going to take. Behind them was a door that appeared to lead to the next train car, but there were no visible handles. There was a bathroom at the rear of the car on the opposite aisle from where Pete and Chris were sitting.

"This is really cool," Chris said. "I can't wait to talk about it on the podcast!" He was looking around the train car and soaking it all in.

A younger guy sitting across the aisle turned to face Pete and Chris. He was in his mid-30s and wore a ball cap that said "Goremonger" on it. "You guys do a podcast?" he asked.

Chris was in the aisle seat and faced him, "Yeah, it's called Heavy Metal Mayhem."

"That's cool. I've never heard of it, but I like listening to podcasts. Mostly true crime, but metal ones, too," he replied. He reached his hand out, "My name is Joey. How cool is this train?"

Pete was listening to the exchange and chimed in, "It is really cool. Is your friend OK there next to you?"

Pete had noticed the skinny young man slumped over with a black cowboy hat on, sitting next to Joey.

Joey laughed. "Ha, don't mind him. That's Mick. He got really drunk last night and never stopped. He passed out on the way here after we stopped for breakfast. It's amazing I was able to get him to the train. He'll be OK after he sleeps off one hell of a whiskey drunk."

Chris and Pete laughed along with him. Mick sat quietly with his head bowed down, a bushy red beard and mustache covered most of his face that could be seen below the hat.

"He loves drinking McCormick whiskey. So, we call him Mick. His real name is Sheldon," Joey added, smiling.

"Well, I guess I'd rather be called Mick than Sheldon, too," Chris said. The three guys laughed at Mick's expense as more passengers began to fill the seats in front of them.

Suddenly a male voice came over the sound system in the train car.

"Please be sure you are in your seats. The 666 Express will be departing the North Dallas train station in two minutes." It sounded like the man that Pete spoke to when he called about the tickets.

"I guess we're about to make history!" Joey said, slapping Mick's knee, causing him to shift slightly in his seat. Mick gave him the middle finger, acknowledging he heard him, but didn't approve. The three laughed again.

The door of the train car closed, and the lights inside dimmed gradually. A distant low hum could be heard on the sound system. It was a deep, guttural noise that seemed to vibrate everything in the car as it got louder. The passengers looked around at each other in confusion as the feeling among them changed from exited to tense.

At exactly 10:30 am the passengers were jerked back into their seats as The 666 Express abruptly pulled out of the station, heading to Denver, reaching 666 miles per hour in less than one minute.

*****

"What the hell is going on?" Pete said, straining his eyes to see outside the darkened window on his side. He took his glasses off and rubbed his eyes. "I can't see a damn thing."

Chris answered, "I don't know. This is pretty crazy. I can't see, either."

The 666 Express continued to move at its incredible speed, but the passengers weren't able to see anything; it was a blur outside through the heavily tinted windows. Pete looked around to see what the other passengers were doing, but most of them seemed to be unconcerned and sitting back in their seats. Some were sleeping, despite the uneasy feeling that hung heavy after the abrupt shutting of the door and low hum that was prevalent on the sound system. Of the 40 passengers that were present in their car, Pete was only able to see four others awake and speaking to each other, in addition to Joey who was sitting across from them. He was talking to Chris about his band, Goremonger, and about the style of heavy metal he played.

The digital sign at the front of the car now only read "666 Express – Make History" with an animated image of fire behind the letters. The low hum that was coming from the sound system continued and gave Pete a very uneasy feeling as he sat back in his seat, trying not to worry about it. He could hear Chris and Joey still talking to each other; it sounded like they were discussing horror movies now. Mick, still passed out, was oblivious to what was going on. Pete felt almost envious of his inebriated state, wishing he were sleeping like the rest, to be awakened in Denver when the train ride was over. The email he got from Diablo Productions said they would have lunch in Denver and take the train back to Dallas at 2pm for a 3pm arrival.

Pete looked at his watch and was surprised to see the battery must be dead. The time showed 10:30 am. It had been at least ten minutes past that now.

"Hey, Chris, check your watch. My battery must be dead."

Chris looked at his and said, "that's weird. Mine is too. It says it's still 10:30."

Pete felt a sense of unease upon hearing Chris' reply. What were the odds that both of their watches stopped at exactly the same time? They asked Joey if he was wearing a watch, but he wasn't. Neither was Mick. Something was not right, but there were no staff in the train car. He didn't see an emergency phone to call the conductor or a staff member. Since the women took their phones, there was no way for anyone in the train car to call, email, or send any message. They even took smart watches with the other personal items. Pete wondered if it was OK for them to get up and possibly try to open the door behind them to go into the second car. There had to be someone they could ask. He was feeling a panic attack coming on.

Suddenly the low hum that was coming through the sound system changed to a heartbeat. It was distant, but there in the background. Pete was definitely not hearing things.

"Do you hear that?" Pete asked. The beating got slightly louder.

"The heartbeats? Yeah, that's really weird."

"I think we need to get up and try to open that door behind us. Something isn't right. I still can't see a damn thing through these windows," Pete said, taking off his seat belt.

*****

Chris and Joey got up from their seats and went to inspect the door that led to the next train car. Pete watched them and nervously looked around to see if any other passengers had noticed anything was strange about this train ride. Chris could tell Pete was starting to panic. While Chris was also concerned, he noticed his friend was breathing harder and starting to sweat profusely. Pete had issues with panic attacks a few years before, when he went through a stressful safety audit and OSHA investigation following an employee at the plant that fell to his death while working in a scissor lift. Despite the fact OSHA did not find the company at fault, the investigation went on for months and caused many sleepless nights. Pete was prescribed medication to deal with the panic attacks, and when the investigation was over, the condition went away.

"It's weird, I don't see any way to open it," Chris said, feeling around the perimeter of the door.

"Maybe the train conductor has to open it or something?" Joey said, looking around for an intercom or some way to let the staff know they needed help.

Chris was now starting to feel the same anxiety as Pete.

"Can you open it?" Pete asked, the stress of the situation showing on his face.

"I don't think so," Chris said.

Chris and Joey sat down. Joey turned to Mick, who was still passed out with his cowboy hat down covering his eyes. "Well, he's not worried about it."

Chris and Joey laughed. Pete kept staring at the digital screen at the front of the train car, which still read "666 Express – Make History". Chris glanced at his watch, which still was frozen at 10:30. He looked over at Pete, who had his eyes closed, taking deep breaths. Chris feared Pete would lose control if things didn't change soon. He also thought they were at least 30 minutes into the trip, so the ride would be over soon. Chris hoped Pete could hold it together for a bit longer, while at the same time, tried his best not to lose control himself as The 666 Express sped down the track at an insane speed. It seemed to be keeping time with the faint heartbeat that was still present through the sound system. He found it odd that no other passengers seemed concerned in the least.

*****

The 666 Express was moving at a tremendous speed and Pete got up from his seat to get the attention of the staff. He figured that there had to be video surveillance in the cars, and someone would see he was moving around in obvious distress.

"I need to do something," Pete said, excusing himself past Chris, "we need to get someone to tell us what's going on."

Chris shifted in his seat, also very concerned, but doing his best to keep it under control.

"How is everyone sleeping through this?" Pete said as he walked down the aisle toward the display screen. He glanced back and forth as he made his way to the front of the car.

Chris and Joey watched him from their seats, unsure of what he was going to do. Both men could tell that Pete looked like he was on the verge of a breakdown.

Pete started beating his hands on the front of the train car, below the screen.

"Is anyone there? We need help!" he screamed out, his fists uselessly pounding the metal wall. No one answered.

Pete turned to face the passengers. They were all slumped over, soundly sleeping as The 666 Express was hauling across the countryside at a breakneck speed. Only Chris and Joey were awake and looking at him. On the left side of the front row there was a young man in his early 20s with a woman about the same age, holding hands while they slept.

"Excuse me," Pete said as he lightly kicked the man's combat boot. The man didn't move after his boot sprung back to its original position.

Pete pushed the man's shoulder. "Hey, are you awake?" The man didn't move!

"I'm telling you something is wrong here! This guy isn't moving!"

Chris and Joey stood up and tried to get the attention of the passengers sitting in front of them. They got the same response as Pete – nothing!

"Holy shit, man! I think these two are dead!" Joey exclaimed, pointing to two women in their 20s in the seats in front of him. "Mick is breathing at least."

Hearing Joey say that made Pete and Chris freeze in place for a moment. They each scanned the passengers before them, and a horrified look swept over both men's faces. Was it possible the entire train car was filled with the dead? The idea of it was shocking.

"What the hell is going on here? Someone has to be playing a joke on us," Chris said as he gingerly walked down the aisle toward Pete. "There's no way these people are all dead!" Sweat was now pouring down his face.

Now all three men were shaking the other passengers to see if anyone else was alive. They got no response.

"Is it just me or did it get a lot hotter in here?" Pete said, wiping the sweat from his face with his shirt sleeve.

"I think it's because we're freaking out," Chris added.

"I don't know. I think Pete's right, it's hotter than hell in here," Joey said.

It had gotten at least ten degrees hotter inside the train car as they sped down the tracks for Denver. Chris, Pete, and Joey didn't realize it, but the trip had been going for 70 minutes.

*****

"I'm not getting a pulse on any of them," Chris said as he hoped his fears were not becoming a reality. Were they on a train full of dead passengers? How did everyone die at once and why were only Pete, Chris, Joey, and Mick still alive? It made no sense at all.

Chris started beating on the front of the train car. "Hey, let us out of here!"

Joey was doing the same thing on the back wall of the

car. No one was answering them.

"I don't know how the hell Mick is sleeping through all this," Chris said, poking at his shoulder to be sure Mick was still alive. The other passengers were seat-belted in and not moving.

Mick stirred then muttered, barely coherent, "what the hell, man?" He resumed snoring quietly.

Beads of condensation were forming on the metal interior of the train car. It was at least 20 degrees hotter inside than it was when the train left the North Dallas Station. All three of the men were drenched in sweat and frantically looking around for a way out of the train car. None of them knew what they were going to do once they got out, but the walls were closing in as they felt an overwhelming sense of claustrophobia. Inch by inch the walls got closer as the seconds ticked by.

Despite the fact Pete was checking his watch every few minutes, hoping it would resume working, it did not. With all the insanity that was going with the train ride, he lost all sense of time and wondered if it had been an hour. With all the bizarre things that happened once the doors closed, and the trip began, Pete was seriously questioning if anything the people at Diablo Productions said was true. Was the entire thing a rouse? Were they all on video for some stupid reality show and this whole train ride a joke for the world to laugh at? His mind was racing, and thoughts were pelting his brain like tiny icicles from a powerful storm.

"We have to do something," Pete said, pacing back and forth at the front of the car.

Chris was looking closer at the digital screen. Condensation had covered the screen as the temperature inside the train continued to climb.

"I hear you," Joey said, who joined Chris. They were trying to pry the monitor off the wall. "This whole train is fucked!"

The hard plastic frame of the screen snapped as the two men pulled the top left corner of it from the metal wall. The screen crackled, then went black.

"Holy shit!" Chris yelled as the screen fell from the broken frame, shattering into tiny pieces on the smooth metal floor.

Pete, Chris, and Joey all peered into a mass of circuits, wires, and connectors where the screen had been. The way it was wired was like no monitor any of them had seen before.

"What the hell is this?" Joey said, pulling one of the wires out to look it. A hot, red fluid spurted from the broken connection.

"Oh my God! Is that blood?" Pete asked as the fluid continued to spray from the broken wire.

"I think it is!" Chris said, trying to crimp the wire, but the pressure was too strong. "I can't make it stop!

Joey suddenly felt something grab the back of his t-shirt. "What the . . . "

A couple that was sitting in the front row had torn off their seat belts and staggered to him, pulling at his shirt. Their eyes were open but vacant. Their pallor was gray and sickly, and low groans came from their mouths. A putrid, fetid odor followed, wafting up as Joey staggered back. Looking past the couple, the other passengers were standing up, some already in the aisles, making their way to the front of the train. He pushed the couple back toward their seats and they fell to the floor, only to stagger back to their feet once again.

Pete and Chris grabbed a piece of the plastic monitor frame, holding them out to defend themselves from the horde of dead passengers. They had been awakened from their slumber of death and were shuffling ever closer. Blood was spraying from the wall where the monitor had once been. More wires had come loose and there was a steady stream running down the wall and to the floor, making it very slippery.

The ever-present heartbeat from the sound system continued to get louder and suddenly distant cries of anguish could be heard. Was it the cries of passengers in the other cars? The noise was unnerving as the three men were grasping at their last strands of sanity among the train car full of dead passengers moving toward them.

As the dead got closer, Joey was backed into the other corner at the front of the car, opposite where Pete and Chris were. Suddenly, he heard a loud voice above the din.

"Fuck all of you!" Mick screamed - now standing up and wide awake. Something had flipped the switch inside his head, and he was in the middle of the chaos with the rest.

Above his head, Mick swung his steel-toed boots by the laces. One in each hand. He was smashing the work boots he had been wearing into the skulls of the dead passengers. They fell in a heap as he hit one after the other with tremendous force, the steel toes making a dull crunching sound against bone.

"Mick! Hell yeah man!" Joey cried out. He was struggling to stay on his feet with the blood sloshing around at the front of the car and the passengers reaching for him.

Pete and Chris were using the broken pieces of the frame to beat back the passengers that were surrounding them. They weren't doing much more than buying time. It seemed like a matter of minutes before they would be overtaken.

Mick continued to swing his heavy steel-toed boots into the heads of the other passengers, knocking them down as he made his way to the front toward Joey.

"Damn! It's about time you woke up, dude," Joey said, thankful his friend was alive.

Joey and Mick made their way to the broken monitor

where Pete and Chris were, and together the men were able to keep the zombies at a distance. Mick continued to swing his work boots and crunch skulls as only a handful of the dead were still on their feet.

The blood was pouring out even faster now. It was hemorrhaging from the gaping hole in the wall as more connections were broken, allowing the bubbling hot blood to gush uncontrollably. Chris, Pete, Mick, and Joey could feel the temperature of the blood increase as it began to burn their feet and lower legs. The level was rising by the second.

The moaning and crying that was coming from the sound system persisted, as did the hideous heartbeat that continued to grow louder. The inside of the train car was absolute madness as Chris and Pete tried to make their way to the spot on the wall where the blood originated. It was burning their skin, but they saw no other way out of the train car. Chris reached up and pushed his hand into the pulsating blood, screaming as the flesh peeled from his hand and arm.

"Hey, I think I found something," Chris screamed as he began to pull sections of the wall away where the wires were coming through.

Pete also began to frantically pull at the wall while Mick and Joey kept the remaining passengers back. The rest were floating in the scalding blood that was now nearly waist deep. The pain was blinding for the men, but they hung on. Chris had one arm completely inside the wall, desperately pulling at whatever he could to get his body into the opening. Pete also had an arm in, doing what he could to find out what was on the other side.

"Hey, come over here!" Pete said to Mick and Joey. There was a large opening in the wall and he was about to crawl through it.

Chris and Pete were pushing through the mass of wires spouting blood with Mick and Joey right behind them. The four men pushed with all the strength they had, desperate to get out of the boiling blood that was rising quickly.

The 666 Express continued to speed along the tracks, going 666 miles an hour, as advertised. It had been three hours since the doors closed and there were four people alive in the first train car. Blood was pouring in by the gallon and had almost completely risen to the top as the men gave one final push into the opening of the wall.

Each man gasped as they hit the floor, barely alive. The skin from their faces was peeling off and their vision was cloudy. The men struggled to see where they had fallen to. They strained to see, yet were horrified at what was there, only an arm's length away. It was a monstrous black heart beating in time with the heartbeat coming through the sound system. The blackened heart was immense, approximately five feet in circumference, throbbing and pulsating before them. It was connected to the rest of the train with what looked like wires, but were veins that carried the blood throughout, feeding The 666 Express. It was a grotesque vision of horror.

"That's so fucking metal," Joey said under his breath in disbelief.

As the men were repulsed at the site of the giant heart beating, what they saw beyond it only added to the insanity of the situation. The windshield of The 666 Express was clear. The nightmarish vision was unlike anything they had ever seen. The train didn't appear to be on train tracks at all. The 666 Express was hurtling at a maddening speed downward through an opening in the Earth and directly into a wall of fire.

The flames were hypnotic and the most brilliant shades of red, orange, and yellow they had ever seen. The maddening sounds inside the train paused and they took a final breath before The 666 Express was swallowed up into the flames, making its final stop in Hell.

Just then a monstrous boom of thunder rang out, and

it began raining blood on the windshield just before everything went black.

Create the Chaos

There was a fine drizzle falling in Danbury, Connecticut. Pete stared out the window that faced west. A boom of thunder could be heard in the distance as a turbulent gray sky loomed. It was a bit chilly for October. He was still wearing dress clothes from the funeral and sipping a single malt scotch with an ice cube as he thought about how much he missed his friend, Chris. It had been one hell of a week. Chris was born and raised in the Danbury area, where he originally met Pete. The rain reminded him of the last trip they took together. The memory brought with it a smile as Pete remembered the crazy nightmare he had about zombies during their train ride. They had a good laugh about it when they returned to the grind of real life. Those were better days.

The door swung open and Joey, Mick, and Shaun walked into Widow's Bar. The rain was falling harder and the wind slammed the door behind them. Shaun shivered since he was not used to temperatures near freezing. They had changed out of their dress clothes at the hotel and were back to jeans and black heavy metal concert shirts.

Mick saw Pete first.

"Hey, man. You didn't drink all the whiskey, did you?" Mick asked, smiling as he sat next to Pete. He put his black cowboy hat on the back of the chair. Mick knew Pete was really down, losing his best friend of more than 20 years.

Pete smiled. "Yeah right. That's YOUR job."

"I can't believe I've been in the States for six hours and I haven't had a drink yet," Shaun said, his Melbourne accent striking in the small neighborhood bar as one of the locals looked in their direction.

A waitress in her thirties came to the table as everyone sat down. She smiled warmly.

"My name is Ellen, what can I get you guys?" she asked.

"Give me a double of whatever he's having," Shaun said, pointing to Pete's glass. "I need something to warm me up a bit."

"Let's get a bucket of Bud bottles," Joey said, Mick nodded.

"Let's have two of those appetizer sampler platters," Pete said, handing her the menu.

"Yeah, that sounds good. I'm starving," Joey said.

"I thought this would be a good place to meet up after the funeral. Chris loved coming here, especially when they had bands," Pete said, looking toward the back room where the local bands would set up.

"Looks a bit small in here for bands, but I'm sure if it was metal, Chris would have been all about it," Mick said, cracking open his first beer. He stroked his bushy red beard.

"Shaun, I can't believe you made it for the funeral. It's so awesome to finally meet each other face-to-face," Joey said, raising a beer up.

Shaun smiled, enjoying a sip of his single malt. "Definitely, mate. I couldn't miss this. Since we've been doing the podcast, I've gotten to know you guys really well. You're a bunch of fuckin' legends."

Shaun was referring to the podcast Pete and Chris started with Mick and Joey after they met on the train ride. It was called *Create the Chaos*, a weekly show about urban legends from all over the world. They added Shaun to the cast after the third episode when he shared legends in Australia, New Zealand, and Tasmania. He was a perfect fit. With the time zone difference, they had to record the podcast on Saturday afternoons so Shaun could do it Sunday morning. The five of them had established a great rapport very quickly, and the podcast was doing better than expected. They decided to keep doing it despite Chris' death. He definitely would have wanted it that way.

"Let's drink to Chris," Pete said as he held up his glass.

"Cheers! To Chris!" they all said, clinking glasses and bottles.

"You know what we should do tomorrow? I mean, Shaun's here in Danbury for two more days, right?" Mick asked.

"Yeah, that's right, mate. I leave Saturday morning," Shaun said.

"We need to take the train to New York City, do a little sight-seeing, and ride the subway to see if we can find that one thing we read about," Mick said.

"Oh, you mean Chaos? That would be awesome," Joey said, wiping the beer foam from his mustache.

Shaun was smiling. "Yeah, that sounds great!"

"I remember reading up on Chaos. You gotta love a monster in the subway system, trapped behind a wall of concrete," Mick said. "It's so bad ass."

"Especially since he's one of the reasons we came up with the podcast name," Joey added.

"Then, let's do it," Pete said, finishing his drink, gazing out as the rain stopped and the sun began to peek from the parting clouds. He smiled and thought of Chris and how it might be a sign of approval.

The four men made their plans to meet at the Danbury train station early the following morning. Mick ordered another bucket of beers when Ellen returned to the table with their food.

*****

1898 - New York City

John McGuire sat down to eat his lunch as the whistle blew. He was the foreman of a sandhog crew tasked to dig the City Hall station for the New York City subway project awarded to the Interborough Rapid Transit System (IRT) company. His uncle Timothy had given him the job to run a 50-man crew. At 33, John was the youngest foreman on the project and did his best to prove to the men he was a worthy leader. Timothy McGuire was the inspector in charge of the project. He was previously the business administrator for the Laborer's Union in New York. There were two other shifts of 50 workers keeping the project going around the clock to meet strict deadlines. None of the men thought of him as anything more than a kid who got his job because of his uncle. They were correct. They did what they were told because he was in charge.

John's slight frame paled in comparison to the muscular members of his crew, and while he lacked in physical stature and experience, John excelled in the art of politics. In a growing city like New York, politics was the only way to move in the right direction. He used his family name to work his way up the ladder. He was a mediocre laborer, but John quickly learned there were other ways to better himself without putting callouses on his soft hands. Being a foreman of the new subway project was like starring in a hit Broadway play.

The laborers were newly coined sandhogs. The name seemed to stick to this hearty group of men who took tremendous risks every day. They followed behind the explosives crew that used dynamite to tunnel into the granite and bedrock over a hundred feet beneath the city's busy streets. While they toiled below ground, the rest of New York hustled and bustled without giving them a second thought. But the subway would revolutionize travel in New York, though the rank and file just didn't know it yet. The sandhogs would haul the debris, dirt, and sand out in buckets to a conveyor belt that took it to the surface after the blasting. It was slow and arduous work to remove only a few feet each day, but the men were paid well for the task, almost double the other trades. Most of them were Irish and Italian immigrants who had a hard time getting into the other unions, but were proud to be sandhogs and bringing home a decent paycheck for their growing Catholic families.

Another sandhog crew was used to tunnel beneath the East River. They suffered casualties from a variety of work place accidents, including the bends, or decompression sickness, where air bubbles enter the bloodstream. In one horrible incident, 27 men were killed when they returned to the surface too quickly. Another accident involved dynamite that went off prematurely, due to a defective fuse, killing 11 and maiming two others. Yet despite this, many immigrant workers were thankful to have a job in a new country where things were more expensive. A strong work ethic and camaraderie got the sandhogs through some long, hard weeks. Drinking alcohol after work helped take the edge off before they got home. Unfortunately, many of them over medicated and became alcoholics.

John's uncle made sure to put him on a project that would pay dividends for his career. To get the job done on time was imperative, since the City Hall station would be the first one of its kind. It was designed by a famous architectural team from London, Teasdale & Schneider, who designed dozens of the most impressive churches in Europe. The mayor wanted to prove New York was the best city in the world. The City Hall station would have a stunning stained glass ceiling that let in natural light from the surface to illuminate the ornate terrazzo and ceramic tile platform. Breathtaking chandeliers, state-of-the-art lighting, and beautiful artwork would adorn the flagship of subway stations. Uncle Timothy was hoping this assignment would catapult his nephew into the stratosphere. He had no sons of his own and wanted to make sure a McGuire was there to take his place when he was ready to retire in ten years.

There were dozens of foremen more qualified than John for such a project, but Timothy didn't care. He was in charge of the subway project and his decision was the only one that mattered; nepotism be damned! This was the first of many parts that would comprise the original subway line. Construction wouldn't officially start until 1900, so this project was kept quiet for the time being. Timothy was using the City Hall station as a means to show off his idea to carve further into the dense granite and bedrock than anyone else. He developed a method he believed would revolutionize the business. Some questioned the safety of using so much explosive with the sandhogs below ground, but Timothy chose to not listen to them. Expert after expert told him it was dangerous. John blindly followed his uncle's ideas.

John finished the last of his lunch as the second whistle blew, signaling the men it was time to resume digging. The shift before them had blasted quite a bit of debris they had to clear away to allow for another section to come down. His crew didn't have to be told to get back to work, they knew that not giving it their best would result in getting fired. These immigrants were not used to better paying jobs in the city and were not going to jeopardize a good thing.

"Hey boss, we're ready to blast," said Silvio, a dynamite crew leader with several years of experience. He was the man who checked the connections of the dynamite and told the sandhogs to move out of the blast radius.

John smiled, knowing that they were about to exceed their daily goal once again for the ninth shift in a row. Using more explosives at the direction of his uncle was the reason for their great progress. Things were going so well, John decided to pack the holes they drilled with even more dynamite. Silvio didn't question him. He knew there were thousands of men ready to replace him. So he did what he was told and hoped things would be OK.

"Great, let's do it."

John watched from a distance as the sandhogs were taking shelter, putting cotton in their ears. They were visible through a narrow opening of the cavern wall. The men wore leather derby caps with a stiff shellacked brim that offered modest head protection. This was years before the hard hat would be introduced in construction and mining operations. Most of them said a silent prayer. The more devout kissed their cross necklaces and rosaries.

"Fire in the hole!" Silvio yelled out, cupping his hands around his mouth. He turned in the other direction and shouted loudly. "Fire in the hole!"

Silvio counted to ten before pushing the plunger of the detonator. There was a massive boom that echoed throughout the area as a torrent of granite and bedrock debris filled the air, causing a massive cloud of dust to permeate the cavernous area. It was louder than the previous blasts and everything shook for a few seconds. A sizzling sound, like a broken speaker, crackled in Silvio's ears. No one dared to look up.

Silvio's hearing was muffled at the time, like it always was following the explosions. Since he was closer to the blast than the rest of the men, he got headaches every night. Silvio's wife, Angela, told him he was losing his hearing, but he didn't believe her. He wasn't 40 yet and refused to believe her claims. Most of the men shared similar stories yet collectively dismissed them. Their families would learn to speak louder in order to be heard.

Despite the throbbing in his head, Silvio thought he heard a horrible shriek in the distance. It was in the direction of the blast but the miasma of dust and debris made it impossible to see anything. He stood silent, waiting for it to sound again. All he heard was his own breathing whooshing in and out. His heart thumped.

"Did you hear that?" asked Billy, a sandhog that was twenty yards away. His face was covered in dust, and he blinked to knock some of it from his eyes.

Silvio couldn't really hear Billy, but he had become good at reading lips. He shrugged his shoulders. He didn't know what the sound could be and didn't want to alarm the others for no reason.

Suddenly the shrieking sound became louder and both men heard it despite their compromised hearing. It was chilling and seemed to come from multiple directions.

"I heard it that time," Silvio said, squinting to see past the dense cloud that continued to billow past them. He coughed in the darkness.

Suddenly, Silvio caught a glimpse of something in the dust in front of him, only a few feet away. It moved very quickly. His heartbeat was reverberating inside him like a stopwatch. Then he saw it again - two huge, yellow eyes with endless dark pupils! Whatever it was had to be gigantic, as the eyes were the size of dinner plates, and it seemed to slither like a monstrous snake. His heartbeat continued thundering in his chest.

Then he heard a sound, like a whisper, from the direction of the eyes.

"Chaos . . . Chaos!" It was hoarse and followed by a low growl that shook the ground. This sent every hair on his body standing and cold shivers cascading across his skin in waves. He felt nauseated.

Silvio turned in place but felt like he was moving in slow motion. Instinctively he wanted to run away. Panic swept over him as his wobbly legs moved like glaciers. *Did he hear it say the word chaos?* He was barely able to get out a yelp when the thing in the dust cloud had him around the face, neck, and chest simultaneously. It felt like hundreds of tiny, clawed hands were pulling at him, squeezing slowly, but with tremendous force. Its rancid breath was hot across his face and reeked of a thousand dead bodies. The beast was dragging him down to the cool rock floor of the cavern. He heard another man cry out before the thing had him down, unable to move, and squeezed him to death.

Then Silvio heard the infernal whisper again. It was more hideous hearing it up close.

"Chaos . . . Chaos!"

A hundred yards away outside of the cavern, John heard the screams. He thought he was imagining them at first, but they were real. The shrieking sound could have been large sections of granite grinding against each other, but the screams were from his crew inside the massive cavern where they had been digging. There were dozens of them now and multiplying rapidly. A foul odor spewed from the opening and John was swept by a sickening feeling.

All his men were inside, and John began to panic. None of them came out like they usually did to get away from the dust. Most wore bandannas around their faces, but it was still difficult to breathe. They used large fans to help move the dust away so they could continue working. But none of that was happening. Nobody was coming out, only horrifying screams and a putrid odor that made him sick.

The hole that led to the cavern was partially covered with a large section of rock that became dislodged and fell in the blast. There was only an area about the size of a child to squeeze out of. John looked in each direction, but there was no one on his side of the cavern. He felt incredibly alone in that moment.

Suddenly a small man came wriggling from the narrow opening. He was covered in dust and fell to the rock floor, gasping for air. It was young Phil Daniels, and it was his third day on the job. The look on his face was one of sheer terror. His eyes were open wide and darting about as he tried to speak but couldn't at first. He made eye contact with John and was surprised to see him standing there.

"W-w-what the h-h-hell is going on, boss?" Phil said, his voice shaky. He normally didn't stutter, but something he saw had him out of his mind with fear.

John didn't know what to say. The two men were only a few feet from each other as Phil gingerly stood up, chunks of debris falling from his clothes. He staggered and grabbed John's arm to avoid falling.

"W-w-we need to go in and s-s-save them!' Phil said looking in disbelief at the narrow crevice he just crawled through. He was breathing heavily.

John didn't know what to say. He pulled his arm away from Phil, who gripped him tightly.

"It was saying c-c-chaos over and over again. C-c-chaos?"

John was trying to process what was going on but Phil didn't seem to be making any sense.

"We can't let that th-th-thing out," Phil said. His eyes were welling up with tears. "It's h-h-huge with giant y-y-yellow eyes."

Both men stared intensely at the entrance to the cavern, the dying screams of the others gave them both a chill. The rotten stench had gotten even worse, wafting from the opening toward them.

John made his way to the large rock that had fallen by

the entrance.

"Come on, let's push this," John said.

Phil paused for a moment and then joined his boss. He didn't know what else to do. Everything was moving in slow motion and his hearing was severely damaged from the blast. His leather cap must have flown off his head at some point since his curly red hair was caked with dust. He was soaked in sweat and trembling.

"Come on, just a bit more," John said, grunting as they tried to move the large hunk of granite into the narrow opening.

The rock shifted suddenly with both men pushing and landed with a deep thud against the makeshift doorway. The two men shoveled gravel on top of it to fill in the small cracks that showed until no one could tell the opening ever existed. It blended in with the rest of the rubble. Whatever was inside was there to stay, and the condemned who remained would be silenced forever.

John and Phil stood there in disbelief as the muffled cries slowly dimmed. The bodies of the 46 sandhogs who died that day were never recovered. Three of the crew were not at work that day due to a stomach bug. The City Hall project continued, drilling in a different direction. The city and IRT didn't want to risk another cave in to recover the dead but instead paid each family $100 for their loss and installed a plaque at the City Hall Station to commemorate their sacrifice for the greater good. The former opening in the rock that led to the cavern was covered in reinforced concrete and finished with mortar and a mosaic ceramic tile pattern to blend in with the rest of the station. Several natural gas and power lines ran in a metal conduit attached to the tile.

John never spoke another word in his life and spent his remaining years catatonic in an insane asylum in Utica, New York. He died from tuberculosis there in 1911. Phil was given a different job with the laborer's union above ground and didn't speak about the events of that day in 1898. Many years later, on his death bed at Misericordia Hospital in the Bronx, Phil confessed what they had done to his wife and two adult children. They intently listened as he told them of the monster named Chaos that was immured in the granite and bedrock beneath New York City. The story became an urban legend among the Irish and Italian immigrant population.

*****

Pete, Joey, Mick, and Shaun sat on the 6 train excited and ready for their New York City adventure. They were on hard plastic orange seats, facing each other, two on either side of the aisle. There were about a dozen other passengers in the car they rode in. Shaun had barely been in the United States a day and was overwhelmed in the busiest city in the world. He had dreamed what it would be like to visit the States and now he was doing everything he could to soak it in. He was taking lots of pictures with his phone. Each side of the car was lined with various advertisements and bright overhead lighting. Heat was coming from metal supply vents since it was unseasonably cold.

They slowed down and the screeching noise got louder. It was metal on metal and shrill. They could hear two loud beeps from overhead speakers as the subway doors opened. They could see the Bleeker Street station sign on the wall. Two passengers got out, three more came in as the doors shut behind them and the subway lurched ahead.

"We're getting close to the Brooklyn Bridge stop. Only a few more," Pete said.

"Man, I still can't believe I'm here," Shaun said, snapping more pictures and smiling.

"Hell yeah! This is awesome," Mick said, taking a few

pictures of his own.

They were riding in the 6 train headed downtown to Manhattan and the Brooklyn Bridge station. Pete found after researching it, that in order to see the now abandoned City Hall Station, they had to duck down to avoid being seen by anyone outside the train as the subway riders exited at the Brooklyn Bridge station. Then as the 6 train made a U-turn to head back uptown, they would be able to briefly see the City Hall Station they read about. It was where the legend of Chaos began in 1898. The subway didn't stop there, but they'd be able to view it through the windows. Each of the men had become obsessed with the lore of Chaos, devouring the stories out there, news articles about the accident in 1898, and more. There were many accounts of the urban legend that Phil Daniels told his family hours before he died of lung cancer. His wife, Samantha, had written about it extensively in a diary before she died in 1955. Pete found a website that published excerpts from her account of what Phil told them. The guys wanted desperately to tell the story about their subway trip to see Chaos on the next episode.

The subway slowed down again as they approached the Spring Street station, then Canal Street. The men were taking in their surroundings as the doors opened and closed. They could see the graffiti on the white tiled walls and knew that Chaos was buried somewhere. At least that's what the legend claimed. It both scared and excited them and they wondered if the story was really true or not. Most of the legends they discussed on the podcast were tales passed down generations, exaggerated each step of the way, like one long game of telephone. But, the chance that maybe one of them could actually be true was the thing they each held onto. There was always a possibility, no matter how small. It made for many interesting conversations on the podcast.

Two years before, Pete and Chris met Joey and Mick

on a train ride from Dallas to Denver. It did seem like an odd coincidence the train was called The 666 Express, and now they were aboard the 6 train below New York. Pete struggled to not think about the similarities. The air brakes hissing and the screeching sounds were all part of the experience. The sensation of being far below ground level was unique. The walls splattered with graffiti were interesting to Shaun, since he was an art teacher and accomplished painter back in Melbourne. Street art was fascinating to him. The local subway riders were scrolling on their cell phones and oblivious to all the noise and visual overload.

"Guys, this is so amazing we're doing this!" said Shaun, taking a selfie with Pete. "I can't wait to talk about this on the podcast."

"Definitely!" Joey said, who grew up in Connecticut but had never ridden the subway.

"Yeah, and it's better that I'm sober enough to be here with you. Not like last time," said Mick, smiling as he pulled his jacket back to reveal a *Mick Nation* flask he kept in his pocket. *Mick Nation* was what he called his "party central" apartment. "I don't leave home without it."

He was wearing the same black cowboy hat he did on their last train ride. Pete noted another similarity.

They all laughed as the 6 train continued on.

"The Brooklyn Bridge station is coming up. Remember what we talked about," Pete said.

The subway slowed to a screeching stop as the doors opened and the passengers got up and left the car. Pete, Shaun, Mick, and Joey stayed behind and once everyone was out, laid down on the bench seats as they discussed. Two beeps sounded and the subway doors closed as the 6 train made its U turn to head uptown. The men knew this was their chance to see the now abandoned City Hall Station.

"This is so cool," Mick said as the subway began to

move closer to the station.

"There it is off to the right," Pete said, pointing.

The City Hall Station was a ghost of its former self, but even in dim light it looked regal. This was to be the crown jewel of subway stations but was barely put into use due to the sharp curve and limited lines to run all the routes. The subway was so successful that the first station was quickly obsolete. So, it was only used for a short time, despite the fact the City of New York spent two million dollars on it.

Pete visualized the crevice buried behind the tiled wall. He imagined what was described by Phil Daniels on his deathbed. When he read parts of the diary, it painted a vivid image in his mind. Phil's descriptions were detailed and visceral.

It was a hideous thing that emerged from the dust and debris in the cavern. We were all blind in the dust, but then we saw it. It was like a huge centipede with the head of a serpent and dozens of legs on each side of its writhing body. It was shiny black in color with piercing yellow eyes that cut through the endless waves of choking dust. It sent a shiver up my spine when I heard it whisper its name, "Chaos". I've heard that evil whisper in my dreams ever since that day in 1898. If I close my eyes, I can see it looking at me.

Just then a monstrous explosion shook the subway car, throwing the men from their seats to the floor. It seemed like it came from a few cars ahead of them. A second explosion was even louder as the subway train flipped over to its left side, forcing the men to hold on to the metal handles. All the lights in the subway went black but thankfully there were some orange emergency lights that blinked, casting the entire car in a strange hue. The flickering made it seem like they were watching the events in an old movie. A distant alarm bell was ringing, barely audible with their muffled hearing.

"What the hell was that?" Joey screamed out. There was a large gash on his forehead and blood was trickling down his face. He wiped it off with his jacket sleeve.

"I have no idea!" Pete said, his left arm ached from where he was slammed against the opposite seats across the aisle. "I think I broke my arm."

Pete could see the pages of the diary in his mind again.

I ran as fast as I could, stumbling and nearly deaf from the blast. Somehow I found my way out. The only person I saw was the foreman, John McGuire. I tried to tell him what I saw but he was shocked by the explosion and all the screaming. The men were being slaughtered by the hideous beast named Chaos. It was squeezing them by the neck, chest and stomach until their heads burst like grapes. It was horrible.

"Where's Shaun?" Mick said, a sharp pain jabbing at his right side. He knew the feeling; it was broken ribs. He injured himself many times as a kid on a BMX bike, jumping ramps with his brother, Michael.

"Over here, guys," Shaun said in response. He was at least ten feet from them, near the doorway that led to the next subway car. "I think I broke my nose, but otherwise I'm OK."

Mick took a swig from the flask. He had been discreet about it, sneaking drinks since they arrived in New York. The McCormick whiskey had that familiar burn going down, but his nerves were on high alert. He took another drink and put it away. He needed to focus on what was happening to stay alive.

Pete wondered if they would hear something from the conductor through the speaker system. Suddenly the doors all sprung open on the right side, which was now above their heads. There wasn't much more light outside of the train. Everything was eerily quiet. The doors on the left side were underneath them and jammed shut from the explosion.

"Shit, should we get out of the car?" Mick asked. He took another drink as he felt his anxiety starting to mount.

"I think we should," Joey said.

One by one the men climbed out of the subway car

through the open doors. Shaun was below helping each one of them. He was the tallest of the group and figured he could get out easy enough.

"I smell gas," Pete said. The familiar smell of natural gas was prevalent as they stood on top of the subway car. His arm was throbbing with pain from the crash.

"Me, too," Joey said.

"Same," answered Mick. "Where's it coming from?"

Shaun was gripping the metal bars inside the subway car, preparing to pull himself up to join the rest when he noticed something moving in the darkness. Immediately he was struck with a horrible stench that filled the subway car. It reminded him of sewer gas. He reached for his phone.

"Hey guys, something's going on down here," Shaun said, as Joey peered inside the car from above. "Smell's awful in here." He snapped a picture.

"What's up?" Joey asked. His face cringed as he could smell the horrible odor. Blood was smeared across his face from the bleeding wound on his forehead.

Shaun looked in the direction of the subway car that was in front of them. The door was open but all he could see was enveloping darkness and the repetitive blinking of the emergency lights. It had a sort of strobe effect. He sensed something was watching him but thought maybe his mind was playing tricks. Maybe all the reading he did about the Chaos legend was getting into his head now?

Suddenly Shaun heard the sound of something moving on the metal subway car floor.

"What the hell?" Shaun said, turning on his phone's external flashlight.

His beam shined into two huge yellow eyes staring back at him! It was in the other car, about halfway down the aisle. He remembered the excerpts from the diary that Pete emailed him.

Those awful yellow eyes still haunt me to this day. In the middle were two pupils, darker than anything I had ever seen before. It was like looking into a bottomless pit of pure evil.

Shaun was frozen in place at what he was seeing. What could he do? Would he be able to pull himself up fast enough, or should he run to the next subway car? Could this possibly be Chaos? He shuddered to think it could be the real thing.

"Chaos, chaos," the monster whispered as it slowly slithered down the aisle, moving like a snake. It was gaining incredible speed.

Shaun started pulling himself up, but his left hand slipped on the metal bar.

"Guys! Help! Chaos is down here!" Shaun screamed as Joey grabbed his right hand, attempting to pull him out of the subway car.

Pete and Mick scurried to the open door, trying desperately to pull Shaun out of the car. How was it possible? Had Shaun really seen Chaos, the legendary beast of the subway?

Shaun felt a tremendous pressure as Chaos grabbed him with four of its long, spindly legs with hairy clawed feet that dug into his flesh. It had him by the ankles, waist, and chest all at the same time, and he began to lose consciousness. The horrible stench that filled the car was its rancid breath. Shaun writhed as Joey, Pete, and Mick had him by both arms, desperately trying to get him out.

Shaun was screaming and blood began to bubble in his mouth. It was horrible to watch their friend getting squeezed to death. Suddenly it jerked Shaun down into the car, nearly pulling them in, too. Shaun was able to let out one long scream before Chaos had him down on the metal floor.

Pete, Joey, and Mick jumped back and then down to the subay station platform. What they had witnessed seemed like something from a horrible dream. They all noticed how the natural gas smell was stronger on the platform. Mick felt sharp pain from his broken ribs with each deep breath he took.

Suddenly the great beast sprung from inside the car, sticking its head out of the doorway. It was a huge black snake head, its forked tongue slithered in and out as it scanned the area. It was on top of the subway car in seconds. Pete, Joey, and Mick were out of their minds with fear. When they saw the horrible yellow eyes, they knew it was Chaos. Every detailed account from Phil Daniels was no exaggeration. Chaos was just as menacing in the flesh as it was in Samantha's diary. The blinking lights reflected in the leathery black skin that covered its body.

By the light of Mick's cellphone, they began to run down the platform. There was some dim emergency lighting on the station walls, but it would have been difficult to find their way without his phone. They ran as fast as they could and noted the gas smell was getting stronger. They dared not look over their shoulders to see if Chaos was behind them. They ran as fast as they could, battered and beaten up from the crash.

"What's up there?" Pete said as the beam of light showed an area of rubble ahead.

"Hell, I'm not sure," Mick said. Amazingly, he still had his cowboy hat on. He winced from the pain in his ribs.

The three men ran up to the pile of concrete and debris from what appeared to be a hole in the tile. There were ruptured metal pipes hanging down; a whooshing sound filled the area. This was definitely the source of the gas smell. Pete knew there were dozens of gas and power lines running through the subway system, but an explosion was the last thing on his mind today. The air was thick with dust and suddenly Mick's light went out.

"Oh shit, my battery just died," Mick said.

Pete glanced back to see if Chaos was coming toward

them but couldn't see anything. He was expecting the creature to already be squeezing them to death like Shaun. The image of that was imprinted on his mind.

"My phone sucks. I don't have a light on mine," Joey said.

"Hang on, let me check mine out. I know my battery was pretty low," Pete said, taking out his phone.

In the dense cloud of dust, Pete was unable to see where Mick and Joey were. He turned around and felt for a place he could walk through, thinking they may have moved around the pile of rubble where he couldn't see them.

"Hey, guys?" Pete said in a whisper, afraid to draw the attention of Chaos. He knew the beast had to be close.

Pete didn't realize that he was no longer on the platform. He was entering a large, cavernous opening. He managed to get his phone out and turned on the flashlight, but his battery was at 15%, so he was hoping to conserve it as much as possible. He was also worried about the gas leak and doing anything that might cause a spark. Shining the light around, Pete couldn't see Mick or Joey. Where could they possibly be?

"Mick! Joey!" Pete's voice echoed in the cavern.

They didn't answer. He began to feel a tremendous sense of dread. Where did Chaos go? He strained to listen for any sign of the beast, but all he heard was silence and the distant sound of the gas leak.

As he moved slowly around the cavern, his light caught a glimpse of something hideous. There were three human skulls, with random bones scattered around them. He continued to shine his light around the space, remarking at how large it was, with a ceiling at least 20 feet above his head. He saw many other skulls with human bones strewn in all directions. He thought about the legend of Chaos and knew he must be in the cavern where the beast originated. Phil

Daniels had been right! The legend of Chaos was real and now he was in a very deadly situation. He wasn't reading about the story in the safe confines of his home any longer.

"Chaos, chaos!" A hoarse whisper came from the far end of the cavern. A low rumble followed.

Pete turned to run but within seconds the horrible beast was upon him. It was at least thirty feet long and six feet in diameter with dozens of legs on each side of its centipede-like body. Its head was massive and resembled a snake with a red forked tongue that darted in and out. He was overtaken by the rotten breath of the hellish monster. Then he felt something grab him by his left foot, pulling him down to the cavern floor.

"Help! Help!" Pete screamed as more of the legs wrapped around his body, squeezing him with tremendous pressure. It tore into his flesh.

The pain was blinding, and Pete screamed out as he thrashed in the grasp of Chaos. It was over in seconds. Pete's lifeless body was thrown down by the beast as it made its way toward the platform. It smelled more human flesh and after a long slumber, Chaos was hungry.

"Joey, did you hear that?" Mick said, looking over his shoulder.

"Yeah, it sounded like Pete. Where the hell is he?"

"Hell if I know. He was here next to us one minute and then he wasn't."

Joey wasn't sure what to think about the situation they were in. Like Pete, the image of Shaun dying at the hands of Chaos was flashing through his mind. Could the legend they read so much about be true? It was hard to see much on the platform as he and Mick made their way around the pile of concrete that spilled out across the terrazzo floor of the City Hall Station and onto the tracks. Mangled subway cars were thrown in every direction. He knew it was the gas explosion that caused the mess. Joey figured that's what let Chaos out.

He suddenly noticed the horrible smell of death they first experienced pouring out of the subway car. Phil Daniels had described that officious odor. Joey could see the pages of the diary in his mind.

It was the worst thing I ever smelled. It was the breath of the beast and the rot of thousands of victims that stayed with him like trophies of flesh and bone. It was hot and sickening, and it permeated every corner of the cavern. It had a strange paralyzing effect on the men, who were unable to do anything when Chaos came to devour them one by one.

"Mick, you there?" Joey asked, his voice wavering slightly.

Joey thought he heard a noise coming from behind him but was petrified to move. Instead he crouched down behind the debris pile. Then he saw something move to his left. It was fast and hard to see in the cloud of dust that hung around the subway platform.

"Chaos, chaos!" A hideous raspy whisper sounded only a few feet away.

"What the . . . " Joey screamed out as he felt something grab his legs. He fell face-first to the hard terrazzo floor, shattering bones and teeth.

Chaos had him down, squeezing without mercy, as Joey let out a garbled cry before blood was spewing from his mouth, nose, and then his ears and eyes. It was a horrible sight as the beast had him by the legs, waist, and chest simultaneously. His head exploded in a red shower of bone shards, blood, and brains.

Mick suddenly turned around and thought he heard Joey cry out. It was muffled. He didn't know how the two of them were separated. His heart thumped in his chest, yet he steadied his breathing.

"Joey!" Mick cried out. He got no response. "Joey! Pete!"

It looked just like the old black and white pictures Pete emailed them. Where were Pete and Joey? Mick wondered if Chaos had gotten to them like it did with Shaun. Would he be next?

Then Mick heard a noise coming from the direction of the debris pile. He wasn't sure what it was, but he feared Chaos coming for him. He considered running, but he knew there was no use.

The next thing he noticed, even stronger than the gas odor, was the rotten breath he smelled earlier when they were on top of the subway car. He knew what that meant. Mick knew what was about to happen and there was only one thing he thought he could do about it.

Very calmly Mick reached into the pocket of his jacket and pulled out the *Mick Nation* flask. He downed the rest of the whiskey and smacked his lips. The disgusting smell of death was getting closer.

"Chaos, chaos," the monster whispered as it slithered closer to the steps of the City Hall Station. Mick could see his huge yellow eyes. Chaos flickered his tongue in anticipation and let loose a deep growl that rumbled the station.

Mick reached for his pack of Pall Mall reds. He sat back, smiled, then pulled out his lighter.

"Yeah, fuck you, Chaos!"

A tremendous boom followed as Mick started a huge natural gas explosion that destroyed a major section of the New York City subway system, taking him and Chaos along with it - blasted into millions of little pieces.

*****

Two Years Later

The City of New York was forced to abandon hopes of rebuilding the subway system that was damaged in the gas explosion catastrophe. The trillions of dollars in property damage and instability of the built-up land mass was simply too costly to repair. What was left of Manhattan was further separated from the Bronx to the north and Brooklyn to the south, much of it sinking down below the water that surrounded it. The bridges that connected the boroughs were destroyed. The Hudson River and East River encircle the now desolate fraction of land that remains. It was renamed Memorial Island as a tribute to the millions of dead that were left behind, the bodies unable to be recovered. Hollow shells of the magnificent buildings that made up the Manhattan skyline are a somber reminder of what once was.

Before the rescue crews left the island, a cell phone was recovered in the subway tunnels under lower Manhattan. It contained several pictures from the 6 train on the day of the explosion. The phone belonged to an unnamed Australian citizen. A four-minute video was also found on the phone that depicted a struggle with a ferocious serpentine beast with huge yellow eyes. The men in the video called the monster Chaos. The phone was confiscated by the US government and the pictures and video were classified as top secret. They were not released to the public or the Australian government so as not to strain relations between the countries.

Many of the Irish and Italian families in New York have speculated that the legendary monster of the subways, Chaos, had something to do with the explosion. It is for this reason that many refer to Memorial Island as Chaos Island and the legend continues to be passed down through generations.

Death Of a Resurrection Man

Resurrectionist, noun. **a person who brings something to life or view again**. A believer in resurrection. Also called resurrection man, a person who exhumes and steals dead bodies, especially for dissection; body snatcher.

*****

The resurrection men would be dead in less than five minutes. Dr. J. Montague Goolsbee and his two accomplices were surrounded by a torch-lit angry mob, armed with clubs and an assortment of sharp objects, at Pittsmoor Cemetery in Sheffield, England. No one would hear their screams as friends and relatives of the recently deceased beat, hacked, and stabbed the three of them to death under a full moon in the small hours of October 31, 1826.

The following is an account of what led these men to their deaths.

*****

Dr. Goolsbee was a difficult person to like. As a baby and young child he seldom drew the love and affection of others, who felt uneasy around the strange boy. He was born James Montague Goolsbee, but went by his first initial and middle name instead. Even as a young boy he would correct anyone who called him Jimmy or Monte. He would wag his finger at them in a mocking way when telling them his name was J. Montague Goolsbee. No one found it cute but instead quite disdainful.

He was the only child of Reginald and Emma Goolsbee of Rotherham, Yorkshire. Reginald was a secondary schoolteacher, and they raised their son in a typical middle-class English household of the late 1700s. He excelled in his studies but was never able to gain a single friend, spending most of his free time reading or conducting scientific experiments. His parents thought it was odd but figured eventually the young boy would grow out of his awkward stage. They made multiple failed attempts to get their son to socialize with other children. They tried to win the strange boy over with a puppy and later a kitten, but he shunned both animals intensely. He even tried to kill the cat twice before they gave it away. Nothing seemed to work. His mother often cried herself to sleep over it.

As a teenager, the odd and peculiar little boy became an even stranger adolescent. His pockmarked, gaunt face with round spectacles made him appear more like an undertaker's apprentice than the doctor his parents wished he would become. J. Montague wore a black suit, white button up shirt, and red tie every day from the moment he awoke until the time he went to bed. He spit-shined his shoes every Sunday night to be ready for the week. He had an oddly deep voice for someone his age, as if he were a smoker after years of abusing his lungs. He was 6-feet-tall at 16 and as thin as a cornstalk, with knobby knees and a slight hunch in his upper back from a spinal condition he developed at birth. He certainly had a face only a mother could love, but even Emma Goolsbee had concerns for her only child. She wanted her front yard to be filled with grandchildren playing outside, but with only J. Montague Goolsbee to sire those children, she feared that would never come to pass. She would be correct in her concerns.

Despite his obvious physical misfortunes and peculiar personality, J. Montague Goolsbee finished at the top of his class in grades and height at 6-foot 4-inches. He also had perfect attendance and was accepted to the University of Sheffield where he excelled in all his classes. Upon graduation, J. Montague went on to their acclaimed medical school and finished at the top of his class. His professors found him strange but were in awe of his abilities. His classmates kept their distance and did their best to avoid him at all costs. J. Montague didn't mind at all because he preferred to be by himself.

Unfortunately, his mother died the summer before he officially became a medical doctor, but his father, Reginald, was very proud his son achieved his goal. He wished his son would find a nice girl and get married, because like Emma, Reginald also longed for grandchildren. With Emma gone, the house was empty and his days in retirement were lonely. Reginald would live to the age of 90 and there would be no little ones to come by for a visit. Instead, he felt only shame and misery at what would become of J. Montague Goolsbee in the years that followed.

Dr. Goolsbee was a fine surgeon with a long list of patients throughout Yorkshire. Though his bedside manner was terrible, his services were always requested at various hospitals. He kept odd hours, but since he lived alone, he bothered no one, and rarely slept. He ate one meal a day with a cup of black coffee in the morning. It was always exactly the same - one poached egg and a piece of dry toast with an apple. He seemed more content sleeping in the day and staying up in the evening, keeping the schedule of a vampire when he could. He seldom slept more than three or four hours.

Though he made a very good living as a highly skilled

surgeon, Dr. Goolsbee was miserly with his money and lived a spartan existence. His only financial indulgence was buying books to fill an impressive library which occupied the entire second floor of his home on Pittsmoor Road on the north edge of Sheffield near the cemetery. It was an old house that spawned many local legends. Stories were told of the creepy doctor who lived alone in a big, haunted house. Oddly, the legends weren't that far from the truth. Once that truth was known to the residents of Sheffield, jokes about the strange doctor didn't seem funny anymore.

As he reached the age of 45, Dr. Goolsbee retired as a surgeon, and began teaching at the University of Sheffield Medical School. The good doctor wanted to shape young medical minds with his knowledge and expertise. He was able to command the highest speaking fees of the medical doctors on staff due to his experience and the fact his lectures were always sold out. He would dissect cadavers and allow students to sit close by to learn what they had previously only known in textbooks. The University of Sheffield knew that keeping Dr. Goolsbee happy was the best way to continue filling their expensive medical school enrollment with the brightest, and most importantly, the wealthiest students. They were in constant competition with other prominent medical schools in London or Edinburgh, Scotland, which had become the epicenter of medical training in Europe at the time. There were also many private organizations providing anatomy classes throughout England.

To attend a lecture of Dr. Goolsbee's, one would not expect the awkward man to command a high speaking fee. His delivery was monotone and haughty, and his voice had so much bass in it that it lulled students to sleep within minutes. It was the freshness of the cadavers that Dr. Goolsbee was able to deliver to the lecture hall that made him a hot commodity to the university. Even his rival, the suave and handsome, Dr. Edward Dillswood, with his impressive London pedigree and vast surgical experience, was not able to put as many students in the lecture hall. Dr. Dillswood had his graduate assistants secretly follow Dr. Goolsbee to find out how he was able to get such fresh bodies to the tables, but no answers came. Only more questions mounted.

Dr. Dillswood wasn't the only lecturer who wondered how Dr. Goolsbee was doing it. They all mocked his grim demeanor and deep monotone voice. Yet they all had tremendous envy at his ability to fill the lecture halls every week. There had been multiple accusations of questionable ethics cast in the direction of Dr. Goolsbee, but no proof was ever given or discovered. The administration of the university was made aware of this on more than one occasion, but no formal inquiries were made. It was as if those at the top of the academic food chain were more than willing to turn a blind eye to whatever methods Dr. J. Montague Goolsbee was utilizing to work his magic. They only saw the bottom line and buried their collective heads, pretending there was nothing of concern with Dr. Goolsbee's character.

What nobody wanted to talk about in the medical field at the time was the practice of using body snatchers or resurrectionists who stole cadavers from cemeteries and sold them to the highest bidder. There was a huge demand for these bodies and a very limited supply. Cadavers coming from executions were divided up by the College of Surgeons. It wouldn't be until 1832 that laws were changed to make more cadavers available for medical research. In the meantime, this created an industry for the dregs of society to take up as body snatchers for the highest bidder. Most of them were lifelong criminals with drinking problems. Gangs of bodysnatchers would follow funeral processions and often fight each other for control of the corpse. They stood to make a good wage doing this and it wasn't illegal at the time, provided they didn't steal any of the belongings buried with the dead. So the jewelry and clothing were often left behind for the more valuable commodity of flesh and bone. The shelf life was brief for those making a living from the dead. Once the bodies were 4-6 weeks old, the doctors weren't interested.

The highest bidders were typically doctors who gave anatomy lectures on a regular basis and charged students an additional fee beyond their tuition to the school. They were in fierce competition with each other and whoever could deliver the freshest bodies on a consistent basis would be the top earner. In the case of the University of Sheffield Medical School that was Dr. J. Montague Goolsbee, the most unlikely doctor to be filling the seats with students. No one knew how he was able to get his bony hands on one or two fresh corpses each week during the fall and spring semester and typically one or two a month for his special summer lectures for other medical doctors who were looking to better their skills as anatomists and surgeons. It was an exciting time in medicine, and these doctors were literally on the cutting edge of discoveries.

Cemeteries were taking stern measures to prevent the theft of their residents by building watchtowers staffed with armed guards or devising mortsafes to cover the graves with heavy steel cages. Some families purchased iron coffins. The wealthy were able to put their dead in mausoleums that could be securely locked up. In some cases, the families and friends of the dead would hide in the woods outside the cemeteries in hopes to catch anyone in the act of resurrecting. These unfortunate body snatchers would ironically end up being sold to doctors themselves for use in anatomy classes but at a discounted rate due to their poor condition.

Dr. Goolsbee turned 46 on October 13, 1824, and that was when he required the services of the resurrection men. He met a rather rough character, Thomas O'Grady, after a lecture he attended on anatomy at the University of Sheffield. He was originally from London but had to move his operation north to avoid some people he had bad business dealings with. The resurrection men had to bribe, steal, and connive their way to getting the cadavers. He was a burly man in his thirties with dark eyes, giant hands, and a flat nose. His curly black hair peered from beneath the cap he wore as he introduced himself, looking around to be sure no one could hear him.

"I can get my hands on bodies, if yer in the market for any, good doctor," Thomas said in a rough but quiet voice, his smile revealing two missing teeth. "Nice and fresh if I say so myself."

Dr. Goolsbee seemed taken aback by the shifty stranger who had overheard him ask a few questions of the lecturer after the seminar was over. Thomas O'Grady was good at looking for perspective clients. He was one of several resurrection men in Yorkshire at the time, though he was new to the area and looking to build his client base.

"I'm not sure I know what you mean, sir," Dr. Goolsbee said, cocking his head slightly and looking through the bottom of his spectacles.

The two men spoke for several minutes, then Dr. Goolsbee scheduled a meeting at his office after normal business hours, so they could discuss the details. After his initial visit, Thomas was instructed to conduct any further business with the doctor at his home on Pittsmoor Road. He made regular weekly visits there when Dr. Goolsbee began performing lectures in January of 1825. The doctor took deliveries of fresh cadavers at 4am each Sunday, when the inquisitive weren't keeping an eye on his actions. He never asked any questions of Thomas O'Grady, who claimed he had arrangements with lodging houses throughout Yorkshire to purchase their deceased tenants. Dr. Goolsbee paid 10 pounds for an adult and 5 for the body of a child, which was slightly more than the going rate. He made a deal with Thomas to not sell his cadavers to any of the other lecturers at the University of Sheffield Medical School.

Dr. Goolsbee quickly learned the coded vocabulary of the resurrection men. An adult was called a large and a child was a small. They also referred to the cadavers as things, so when they were discussing business, it wouldn't be easy to decipher their true intent. While it wasn't illegal, the resurrection men were not looked at in a positive way, nor were the doctors who paid for their services. Families of loved ones were furious when graves were violated, and it often led to violence. The best of the resurrection men were able to stay far from the purview of the police and grieving families to earn a good living. The problem with most of them was their love of drinking alcohol, which was often the reason they got into fights and were thrown in jail on a regular basis. Or worse, they would get drunk and tell the wrong person what line of work they were in.

Dr. Goolsbee secretly found it rather exciting to be in the resurrection business, despite his dislike of Thomas O'Grady. He considered the man uncouth and disliked the way he stunk of cheap cigars and body odor. In contrast, Dr. Goolsbee took two baths each day and always kept himself impeccably clean. He neurotically washed his hands on the hour, no matter what he was doing. His house was so well kept, the few visitors he had doubted anyone actually lived there. The doctor was making a lot of money with the arrangement, so he considered Thomas O'Grady an acceptable burden. He did greatly enjoy getting under the skin of his rival, Dr. Dillswood, who continued to send his assistants to follow him home from work or watch from the woods that surrounded his home.

For the first six months of their arrangement, Thomas was able to provide him with fresh cadavers, and things were going well at the university with his lectures. For two consecutive weeks in May of 1825, Thomas failed to bring any cadavers for his usual Sunday morning drop off. This was a concern since the semester was almost over and he was hoping to finish his lectures strong. The last thing he wanted was any of the other doctors to surpass his attendance records.

The doctor was concerned about looking into the services of the other body snatchers. It might draw unwanted attention. He knew there were several resurrection men in Yorkshire, but he didn't want to talk to the other doctors about how they were getting their cadavers. The university had to fill the lecture halls with fresh flowers and spices to disguise the smell of the decomposing bodies. They used fans and did what they could to mask the unpleasant odor. The worse it was, the fewer students signed up. Using other resurrection men would mean having to settle for substandard research cadavers that were much more decomposed. It would also put him at tremendous risk for those who were following his every move, like Dr. Dillswood and his brood of assistants. He needed to keep his methods all to himself. It was better that he wait and hope Thomas would return in time for the summer lecture season.

It was July of 1825 and Dr. Goolsbee had given up on the resurrectionist, Thomas O'Grady. He believed the ruffian had gotten himself in trouble with the law and was in prison, or possibly discovered retrieving a corpse and murdered by an angry group of family members. In either case, Thomas was no good to him, and he needed to do something. The university did obtain a few cadavers from the College of Surgeons, but those were divided between lecturers. It wasn't enough, and he noticed a decline in his attendance as compared to when Thomas was bringing him a fresh body each week. It was impacting his earning potential and concerned him a great deal. Especially now that he was fully retired as a surgeon and only working at the university.

An idea came to Dr. J. Montague Goolsbee when he was eating his breakfast one morning that July. It would change his life dramatically. Oddly, it was the resounding snap of a mouse trap he set behind the stove that became his muse. He had seen the disgusting creature scurry across his immaculately kept kitchen floor for a few days and was furious over it. He vowed that he would kill it and rid his house of the vermin. He rarely saw mice at the house despite the fact he was surrounded by woods. He refused to get a cat like most people did who lived in the country. He despised them since childhood and didn't think they were much better than having a mouse in his home.

He jumped up from his seat at the kitchen table when he heard the trap was sprung. In a rare showing of emotion, the doctor was giddy with excitement.

"I got you, you little bastard!" Dr. Goolsbee said, setting his coffee cup down.

He cautiously peered behind the stove where the mouse trap was sprung and was pleased to see the small brown mouse dead, its legs stretched out and tiny mouth slightly open. A small amount of blood was on the floor where the metal trap landed on its vile head. It disgusted Dr. Goolsbee, but he was happy the creature was deceased, and he used an old rag to pick up the trap and clean up the mess. After he threw it away in the garbage can outside, he washed his hands twice and sat back down to finish his coffee. That's when the idea came to him.

The idea was a culmination of his need for more cadavers, his incredibly frugal nature, and the desire to outdo the other professors, namely Dr. Dillswood. Rather than waiting around for the irresponsible and unsavory resurrection men, Dr. Gooslbee would take matters into his own hands - literally! Well, not exactly. He would need some help to pull off his plan, but if things went just right, he would have a steady supply of cadavers for the last part of his summer lecture series and into the foreseeable future!

*****

One month later

It was the night of August 5th, 1825, and Dr. Goolsbee sat in his office at the University of Sheffield. He tapped his right forefinger on his desk and stared out into the night through a small window. For a Friday, he was there much later than usual. It was just before classes started up again, so there was no one around. Earlier he met with two of his graduate assistants that were recruited specifically for this new idea which came to him when the mousetrap was sprung a month before.

The first one that came to mind was a brilliant young medical student from Germany, Louis Friedhof. He was a rotund young man who was barely 5-foot 6-inches tall with curly blond hair he kept short. His English was excellent, though he had a striking German accent. Louis was studying in England as part of a gifted student exchange and was lodging in a two-story home the university owned for international students. His family back in Germany were dairy farmers and struggled to pay his tuition, so he was very grateful to have a job with Dr. Goolsbee. He came from a large family of eight children and grew up doing hard physical labor on the family farm. It was unusual that he was so chubby working on a farm, but he ate like three young men and packed on the extra weight since he was studying in England. He was not about to ruin his chance to earn his doctor of medicine free of charge at a reputable school as the University of Sheffield. Louis didn't flinch when he found out what Dr.

Goolsbee expected him to do.

The other graduate assistant was the opposite physically of Louis. Ian Michael Grimm was a thin, tall young man who was originally from the working-class city of Birmingham. He was nearly as tall as Dr. Goolsbee, and the rings around his eyes and gaunt face would make a person wonder if the two were related. He also wore round-rimmed glasses and kept his brown hair slicked back like the professor. Ian was very intelligent and came from modest means, spending his teenage years in an orphanage since his parents were killed in a terrible fire at the textile factory where they both worked.

Ian excelled in his studies and made it to the University of Sheffield on a scholarship. Four years later, he was accepted in the medical school because of his excellent grades and work ethic. Like Louis, Ian needed the job working as a graduate assistant to pay his medical school tuition. Dr. Goolsbee thought Ian was a good choice to work with Louis on this special assignment that paid more than any of the other graduate assistant positions. As cheap as Dr. Goolsbee was, he was willing to pay for their silence and agreement to do the job he asked. Due to the scope of their duties, Dr. Goolsbee was funding their salaries himself.

Upon their graduation, Dr. Goolsbee planned to release them from the agreement and give both glowing letters of recommendation. Ian was surprised when Dr. Goolsbee explained what they would be doing, but seemed fine with the arrangement, nonetheless.

Dr. Goolsbee purchased a horse-drawn carriage that was used for the transportation of ice at the time in England. He bought it from an old farmer who was retiring and selling the horse and carriage to fund a move to Ireland. The back of it was insulated and fully enclosed instead of an open passenger compartment. Louis had experience with horses from his family farm in southern Bavaria, which was helpful.

He also purchased uniforms for the two young men, and re-painted ICE on the sides of the carriage and across the rear double doors. This would be the perfect cover for what he had in mind.

Two patients owed Dr. Goolsbee money for medical services rendered, and he used the money to purchase the horse and ice carriage. There was paint left behind at his office after some work the maintenance crew completed before he moved in. He brought it home to do the job. The ever-resourceful Dr. J. Montague Goolsbee was able to pay for everything, including food for the horse with money that was owed to him and some leftover white paint. The money he would save not having to hire the services of the resurrection man was more than enough to divide between Louis and Ian with a little leftover for himself.

Ian and Louis left to go out and perform their debut mission while Dr. Goolsbee sat in his office, gazing nervously out the window. Both men were sworn to secrecy, and since the doctor had the upper hand on each, given their need to earn money to complete their MDs, he felt the risk was minimal. Plus, he would not be with them and could just deny any involvement. The doctor would say he hired the two men to deliver ice and nothing more. There would be some ice in the carriage to make the whole thing appear legitimate.

*****

Ian and Louis sat in the ice carriage waiting in an alley off Broomhall Street, just as Dr. Goolsbee had told them to do. They had been there about 30 minutes on a humid August night. Their instructions were very clear. They had rehearsed the details many times.

"How long do you expect we'll have to be here? It's a warm night," Louis said, peering from beneath the brim of the hat he wore as part of their uniform. His stomach grumbled from not eating dinner before they left.

"I'm not sure, mate," Ian said, "I guess as long as it takes."

Suddenly a prostitute staggered down the lit street into the darkness of the alley. She wore a red and black dress, gray stockings, and ankle-high boots. The dress seemed too small for her full figure, and her breasts were peeking out the of bustier she wore. Dr. Goolsbee told them prostitutes were common in that area of town. There were two cheap lodging houses nearby the women rented by the hour to satisfy their customers. Dr. Goolsbee explained prostitutes and homeless people were ideal targets, since they were transient by nature and less likely to be missed by loved ones.

"Hey lads, you looking for some company tonight, are you?" the woman asked. She was missing two teeth and looked like she was at least twice their age. "The name's Holly." She had a slight slur in her speech and her breath reeked of alcohol. She placed a hand on the carriage to steady herself.

Ian smiled. He was the designated spokesman of the two.

"Well, yes we are, madam!"

"Both of you?"

"Yes, give him your hand," Ian said.

Louis helped her onto the front bench seat of the carriage as Ian took out a flask of whiskey that Dr. Goolsbee gave them. He handed it to Holly, who seemed surprised they offered it to her. She was used to selling herself for a few quid if she was lucky. Just enough to pay her food, lodging, and to drink herself to sleep with the strongest whiskey she could find. Anything to dull the pain of her existence. After losing two children in a house fire and a husband to a farming accident, she had nothing to live for.

"Don't mind if I do, boys," Molly said, taking a long pull from the flask. It burned going down, but she liked it that way. It took her mind off the pain for a few moments.

Ian and Louis watched her take a long drink. They both sized up the older woman and thought about what Dr. Goolsbee told them to do. They rid their minds of any sympathy, thinking of it in a positive way - like shooting a horse with a broken leg. Dr. Goolsbee put it to them both that way. In his mind, the doctor thought about the unlucky mouse in his kitchen and how he put the disgusting thing out of its misery.

"No problem at all, miss. Drink as much you want. We've got plenty more," Ian said, grabbing a hold of her by the left arm while Louis took the right.

The two men quickly had her down on the floor in front of the bench seat. In seconds Ian placed his hand over her mouth to stifle her screams, and with his other hand, pinched her nose shut. Her eyes were open wide in terror at the realization of what was happening to her. She wanted to breathe but was unable. Before Holly could escape, Louis sat down on her chest. He used his girth to pin her to the floor. Her legs flailed but soon lost their power as Ian's steady grip on her nose and mouth suffocated the woman. Within a couple of minutes, she lay lifeless on the floor of the carriage. It went easier than both men imagined.

In the darkness of the alley, the men placed Holly in the back of the carriage behind a row of large ice blocks. They covered her body with burlap sacks, so no one would be the wiser, should the roving eye of a policeman peer inside. All of this was part of their instructions from the doctor.

Without another word they rode the carriage out to Dr. Goolsbee's home on Pittsmoor Road by the old cemetery. Ian whistled an old English drinking song and then sang quietly as they made their way down the cobblestone streets of Sheffield.

The hooves of the horse seemed to keep him in time.

Come all ye bold fellows that have to this place come
And we'll sing in the praise of good brandy and rum
Let's lift up our glasses, good cheer is our goal
Bring in the punch ladle, we'll fathom the bowl.

*****

Once the young men arrived at Dr. Goolbee's home, they were instructed to pull the carriage around back to a small barn on the north side of the property. Once inside, Ian and Louis picked up the body and placed it in a small room the doctor had them build the week before. It was lined with bales of hay and there were blocks of ice inside, where the cadavers would be stored inside large burlap sacks.

"So, how did it go?" Dr. Goolsbee asked in the dim glow of a lantern he carried.

"Just as you said it would, sir," Ian said.

Dr. Goolsbee responded with a thin smile. That was the most emotion one could expect to see from him.

This would conclude the first mission of Ian and Louis. As expected, the men followed Dr. Goolsbee's instructions flawlessly. They were paid the fee agreed upon and were on their way back to the university to sleep after a busy night out. Dr. Goolsbee locked up the small room in his barn and walked back to the house, washing his hands twice before retiring to bed. He was very pleased.

Each of the men found it difficult to fall asleep after what they had done. There was no turning back now.

*****

Over the course of the next eight months, Ian and Louis managed to repeat the same procedure an astounding 18 times in Sheffield and some of the surrounding towns in Yorkshire. Dr. Goolsbee had plenty of cadavers to astound his students, the other professors, as well as the administration. It didn't seem to bother anyone the bodies were so fresh and showed none of the telltale signs they were snatched from the grave. After all, it was Dr. J. Montague Goolsbee that was receiving the bodies, and the two graduate assistants would help him prepare them for dissection. The bodies showed no obvious signs they had been murdered. There were limitations on what a medical examiner could discern when the cause of death was suffocation. No one was asking questions of Dr. Goolsbee or the other professors to benefit from plausible deniability. They were all using the services of resurrection men at Sheffield University and throughout Europe. Everyone except Dr. Goolsbee. He was his own resurrection man, and his hubris was growing by the day.

He was even starting to smile a little more, especially when he thought about how much money he was making. Yet beyond the benefit of the financial gain, Dr. Goolsbee was getting under the skin of his nemesis, the handsome Dr. Edward Dillswood. Part of it was a release of the pent-up up anger he had growing up looking like he did in a world so cruel and obsessed with facade. Not to mention the way his own parents shunned him, trying desperately to force him to do things he didn't want to, instead of loving him for who he was. For the first time in his life, Dr. Goolsbee felt alive and at the top of his game.

It was April of 1826 and there was one month left of classes. There were two cadavers on ice in the barn and Dr.

Goolsbee calculated he would need four more to get him through to the fall semester. At the rate Ian and Louis were going, they could easily get that done and he would give them a month off. He wanted to pay them well and give them some time to themselves. He needed Ian and Louis to keep this operation going like it was. It was a cost of doing business, and without them the whole thing would collapse.

Dr. Goolsbee felt confident when it came time to negotiate his speaking fees in June, that he would be able to increase them 25% or more. He was shattering any attendance records the university had ever seen for the anatomy and dissection lectures. They had to move him into a larger hall that was typically used for large assemblies at the school. If things continued like this, he would be able to retire at 55 and live comfortably on his savings, investments, and the university pension. He thought maybe he would like to travel the world and speak at select medical conferences to stay relevant. Possibly write an autobiography.

Dr. Dillswood was beside himself with jealousy. He secretly met with three of the other professors in the department to disscuss the peculiar Dr. Goolsbee. They all knew the small circle of resurrection men that the professors used and none of them were working for Dr. Goolsbee. They knew he had to be up to no good but there was not a shred of evidence to prove it. He gave Dr. Dillswood the creeps from the first time he laid eyes on the strange gaunt man with dark rings around his eyes and an almost gray pallor. The slight hunch in his back added to the mysterious look of the doctor in black. The professors all laughed when Dr. Dillswood referred to Dr. Goolsbee as an undertaker and joked he looked more like a cadaver than the bodies he was dissecting. The truth was, Dr. Dillswood was furious, and he couldn't figure out what to do. The other professors didn't offer any suggestions. It was beginning to have a serious impact on his sleep, marriage, and overall demeanor. The usual suave and sophisticated doctor was starting to unravel.

The entire staff of professors used their capable graduate assistants to follow Dr. Goolsbee around in a discreet way. They worked in shifts, with someone keeping an eye on him as much as possible. On several occasions they observed Dr. Goolsbee's house from the dense woods that surrounded it. It was set off from Pittsmoor Road about 800 meters, down a winding gravel driveway lined with large oak trees. They couldn't get close enough to see him once he went inside, and he rarely left the house. The curtains were always drawn tightly.

Dr. Dillswood talked to his wife, and she suggested he go see the police chief, Captain Ned Howell. Ned was a sensible man and they knew each other well. They attended church together and had children about the same age.

"Ned, there's something strange going on. I need you to do me a favor," Dr. Dillswood said, drinking a pint of beer with the police chief at a local Sheffield pub.

He went on to tell Ned his suspicions about the cadavers that Dr. Goolsbee seemed to always have on hand.

"I can have my men take a look around and see what we can come up with," Ned said before he finished the rest of his pint. He smacked his lips.

Dr. Dillswood smiled and ordered them two more.

"I appreciate it. I think if you dig hard enough, we just might find out what Dr. J. Montague Goolsbee has been up to for more than a year."

Both men laughed.

*****

A week after the meeting between Dr. Dillswood and Captain Ned Howell, Dr. Goolsbee began to notice a stronger police presence around the university. They seemed to be spending quite a bit of time at the medical school, speaking to the other professors, secretaries, and administration. Dr. Goolsbee found it odd that none of the police officers came to talk with him. He began to fear that something or someone had tipped them off about his operation. Dr. Goolsbee felt confident that Ian and Louis had not revealed their secret, especially since it would lead them both straight to the gallows for committing the murders.

He had a rehearsed story ready should anyone ask him about where he was getting the fresh bodies. He would make the claim that Thomas O'Grady did. He would say he had arrangements with the lodging houses to get their cadavers, since they were typically dealing with older citizens, the poor, transients, and people who were drinking themselves to death. The truth is, he did have arrangements with them to pick up their dead, and he was giving them a finder's fee for the business. Dr. Goolsbee had woven quite the web to cover bases should questions come up. He expected they would eventually and wanted to be prepared. He also had Gregory Q. Marlette, the best solicitor in Yorkshire, on retainer should the need arise.

One night at his house, Dr. Goolsbee thought he saw a man coming up his driveway on foot. The doctor was sure he saw someone, but no one was there moments later. The following morning Dr. Goolsbee was eating his breakfast at the kitchen table and thought he saw a policeman gazing into his window. When he jumped up to get a better look, the man was gone and nowhere to be found. He was certain he saw the man.

Dr. Goolsbee was concerned about the shortage of cadavers with two more scheduled lectures before the end of the semester. These were attended by students who paid extra for the chance to dissect a cadaver for themselves, and the doctor would make a lot more money. These worries were affecting his sleep and he found himself looking out the windows often. He decided it best to not send Ian and Louis out for a little while just to be certain he was not under investigation. He would use the cadaver on ice in the barn for the last two lectures and hope the men could resume their activities soon. He hated to keep Ian and Louis idle, but he knew it was far better than the police finding out about what they had been doing. They would all hang for their deeds, including Dr. J. Montague Goolsbee. Even worse than a death by the hangman, would be publicly tarnishing his impeccable name. He knew Dr. Dillswood would enjoy that entirely too much.

Reading the Sheffield Daily Telegraph the following day, Dr. Goolsbee found a notice that an 62-year-old woman, Mrs. Abigail Peterson, had died of natural causes at her home in nearby Doncaster. What caught his eye was the mention that the services would be at Pittsmoor Cemetery on October 3oth. That was the graveyard down the road from his house. They didn't seem to bury people there often. In the 20 years he had lived nearby, Dr. Goolsbee only could think of a handful. There were cemeteries closer to town that were more commonly used. The article went on to say there were many Petersons buried at Pittsmoor Cemetery and Abigail would be placed in the family plot on the north end.

Dr. Goolsbee wondered if any of the resurrection men would come out to the old cemetery to try and retrieve Mrs. Peterson after the burial. There were no watchtowers or night guards on duty there. He never observed the popular mortsafes some families were using to keep the body snatchers away. Dr. Goolsbee thought about it while he drank his black coffee that morning. He stared out the window and thought about his next move.

Two days later the answer came while he drank his

morning coffee. There was an article in the newspaper that made the doctor smirk. Abigail Peterson was the daughter of a retired policeman with the Sheffield department and there would be many of the top brass from Sheffield and the surrounding towns at the funeral. Dr. Goolsbee knew that the family member of a retired police officer would be the last person a resurrection man with a brain would pursue. This just might be the perfect opportunity for him to swoop in and have his assistants get Mrs. Peterson.

Dr. Goolsbee had Ian and Louis meet at his house the day after the funeral. As the newspaper predicted, there was quite the procession the day before at the cemetery for the burial of Abigail Peterson. Every police officer in the surrounding area was at the funeral. Her son was very respected as a police sergeant in Leeds, and her father was well known throughout Yorkshire, even in retirement. Now that all of that crowd was gone, the old cemetery was nice and quiet once again.

It was 11pm on October 31, 1826, and Dr. Goolsbee sat at his kitchen table with Ian and Louis. They were all dressed in black.

"I've decided to go with you tonight," Dr. Goolsbee said, looking sternly at both.

"Really? Are you sure that's a good idea, doctor?" Ian said.

"Yes, I think it would be best for me to be there as a lookout. You'll both be busy digging. But with the fresh earth, I expect it shouldn't take you both an hour to have the casket open. You might need me to help you get her out of the hole, depending on how deep it is."

Dr. Goolsbee was sure to give them both a detailed plan of what was about to transpire. The fact he was going with them was a new spin on the system that had worked well before. Louis was concerned that they were doing things differently and had some religious reservations about digging up the dead. Oddly, he seemed fine with murdering 20 people by sitting on the unsuspecting victims while Ian smothered them. The hypocrisy was rich.

They drove the ice carriage to the cemetery and parked it in a cluster of trees that Dr. Goolsbee scouted out days before. The horse was tied up. It would be difficult to explain why two young men delivering ice would be at a remote cemetery at midnight. If things went as planned, Dr. Goolsbee felt they would be able to get Mrs. Peterson to the carriage and have her on ice in the barn before anyone would miss her.

It didn't take them long to find the burial site on the north end of the small cemetery. In the cool October air, there was a thin fog that blanketed the area. Ian and Louis brought the shovels and began the slow work of unearthing the corpse. Every sound seemed magnified at midnight in such a desolate place. Ian paused for a moment, thinking he heard a noise coming from a wooded area on the west side of the cemetery. It gave him the chills being there at night like this. While he wasn't as religious as Louis, it seemed terrible to desecrate the grave. Especially under a full moon that beamed overhead.

Dr. Goolsbee noticed that the shoveling was making more noise than he planned for, as each shovelful of dirt was mixed with gravel. This was a common method which cemeteries used to act as an alarm that someone was digging where they shouldn't be. He knew there were no houses closer than his, so he wasn't concerned someone would hear the shoveling. It just surprised him, despite the fact the men were being careful, they were making a lot of noise.

Several shovelfuls later, Louis stopped.

"Did you hear that?" he asked.

Dr. Goolsbee was staring off to the west. He heard it, too, and held up his hand to motion them to stop what they were doing. It sounded like a branch snapped. With the shoveling ceased, it was distinct.

"Stay still, gentlemen," Dr. Goolsbee whispered, holding his forefinger to his lips as he crouched down to a knee, surrounded by the fog.

Ian and Louis did the same. They waited silently with Dr. Goolsbee as the night seemed to swallow them up. The full moon above cast the entire scene in a strange yellow hue. They could sense eyes watching them from somewhere in the west. The feeling was unnerving!

Another branch broke, this time from the north side. It was much closer. The three men were crouched down below the fog, hoping it would make them invisible to whatever was hunting them. It felt like they were being stalked. Each of the men had the same sensation. Now, as another branch broke, they felt a presence in the darkness inching closer.

Dr. Goolsbee looked over his shoulder at Pittsmoor Road and the area where they hid the horse and carriage, but it was concealed by the blanket of fog that seemed to be thickening as the minutes ticked by.

Suddenly the north end of the cemetery was illuminated, and the three men stood up, dumbfounded at what was going on. They shielded their faces from the fiery glow coming at them from all sides.

"We would advise you men to stop what you're doing," a male voice said. He was holding a torch and walking toward them from the north.

The three men looked to the west as others were coming toward them with lit torches, the fires flickering as they closed in. There were a lot of them and they meant business.

Dr. Goolsbee could feel his heartbeat thundering in his chest. *How could this be? How long had these men been hiding in wait?*

"I am Dr. J. Montague Goolsbee, and these are my

students. We are here on university business," the doctor said with a nervous confidence. His voice wavered and was ignored by the group as they moved closer.

"And we are the friends and family of Mrs. Abigail Peterson. We are here to put a stop to what you heathens are doing. You will not desecrate this grave tonight, Dr. Goolsbee!"

Slowly a crowd of forty friends and family closed in on the three, their faces covered with disgust and hatred for what they were witnessing. They had been warned the resurrectionists would come to retrieve another cadaver. But they didn't believe it until they saw it with their collective eyes. These men were armed and ready to exact revenge on the bodysnatchers. Most of them were men of the law that were not at the cemetery in an official capacity. They were judge, jury, and executioners on this night. They would remain anonymous and not speak of what was about to happen.

Dr. Goolsbee, Ian, and Louis closed ranks, knelt, and shook - arms interlocked to shield themselves from the impending attack. Bones crunched and blood soaked the ground as the men were pummeled with axes, knives, clubs, and bare fists until they would become fair game for the resurrection men or wild animals - whichever claimed their wretched bodies first.

"And my 'prentices will surely come and carve me bone
from bone.
And, I, who have rifled the dead man's grave, shall never rest
in my own."
*1822 advertisement for Bridgman's Iron Coffins, The Surgeon's
Warning*

Acknowledgments

I would like to thank to some people who helped make this book possible. I always like to point out those who work behind-the-scenes. I truly appreciate every one of them!

My wife and editor, Jenny, for doubling as a beta reader as well as my editor. As I mentioned in the introduction, she was the spark for the idea to publish this series. She does a great job helping to tighten up the words I crank out and provide a good eye for grammar and punctuation. You know that stuff we were SUPPOSED to learn in school?

Artist and friend, Brian Uziel, who creates the artwork that draws in the readers when they pick up a book at one of my appearances. I get compliments on the covers often, and I appreciate his incredible talent. It was his idea to incorporate a grindhouse style to the artwork for the *Slab of Sickness* series and we plan to continue using that concept.

My beta readers and friends, Shaun Farrugia, Rebecca Bohmsach, and Shane Borczuch, who give me feedback on the rough drafts with honest constructive criticism. I often ask them things about the stories, such as, "were you surprised when Joe opened the door" or "did you expect Aunt Edna to turn into a demon"? Stuff like that helps me know what's working and what's not. I like to surprise you, so beta readers are a very important weapon to any author.

Last but certainly not least, thanks to all the readers who enjoy my writing. It's you guys that really make this enjoyable. I can't tell you all enough how much I appreciate it. I hope there will be more of these *Slab of Sickness* books in the future.

About the Author

Pete Altieri lives in a small Central Illinois town with his wife, Jenny. He's the author of the *Creation of Chaos* short story collections, and the novels, *Deeper Than Dead*, and *The Dreadful Lives of Enoch Strange*. Pete's short story, *Man With Spots*, was a finalist in the 2017 TNT network horror contest.

Pete is also the writer, producer, and co-host of the weekly *Murder Metal Mayhem* podcast.

Follow Pete on Facebook and Twitter

PeteAltieri.com

PETE ALTIERI
DEEPER THAN DEAD
ARTWORK BY BRIAN UZIEL

PETE ALTIERI
THE
DREADFUL
LIVES
OF
ENOCH
STRANGE

www.ingramcontent.com/pod-product-compliance
Lightning Source LLC
Chambersburg PA
CBHW072030150726

47999CB00002B/830